THE KING OF KINGMAN
THE STORY OF A MAN WHO CHANGED THE WORLD

KENNETH KAGE

Copyright © 2021 Kenneth Kage.

All rights reserved. No part of this book may be used or reproduced by any means, graphic, electronic, or mechanical, including photocopying, recording, taping or by any information storage retrieval system without the written permission of the author except in the case of brief quotations embodied in critical articles and reviews.

This is a work of fiction. All of the characters, names, incidents, organizations, and dialogue in this novel are either the products of the author's imagination or are used fictitiously.

Archway Publishing books may be ordered through booksellers or by contacting:

Archway Publishing
1663 Liberty Drive
Bloomington, IN 47403
www.archwaypublishing.com
844-669-3957

Because of the dynamic nature of the Internet, any web addresses or links contained in this book may have changed since publication and may no longer be valid. The views expressed in this work are solely those of the author and do not necessarily reflect the views of the publisher, and the publisher hereby disclaims any responsibility for them.

Any people depicted in stock imagery provided by Getty Images are models, and such images are being used for illustrative purposes only. Certain stock imagery © Getty Images.

Scriptures taken from the Holy Bible, New International Version®, NIV®. Copyright © 1973, 1978, 1984, 2011 by Biblica, Inc.™ Used by permission of Zondervan. All rights reserved worldwide. www.zondervan.com The "NIV" and "New International Version" are trademarks registered in the United States Patent and Trademark Office by Biblica, Inc.®

ISBN: 978-1-6657-0976-7 (sc)
ISBN: 978-1-6657-0974-3 (hc)
ISBN: 978-1-6657-0975-0 (e)

Library of Congress Control Number: 2021914383

Print information available on the last page.

Archway Publishing rev. date: 12/29/2021

FOR DONNIE

CONTENTS

Chapter 1   The General 1

Chapter 2   The Murder 5

Chapter 3   Going Home 21

Chapter 4   The Next Day 25

Chapter 5   The Park 35

Chapter 6   The Crime Scene 43

Chapter 7   The Chase 47

Chapter 8   The Data Is Reliable 55

Chapter 9   The Killer's Mistake 65

Chapter 10   The Professor's Discovery 69

Chapter 11   Forbidden 73

Chapter 12   Universal Computer 77

Chapter 13   Preparing for the Trial 83

Chapter 14	The Arraignment	87
Chapter 15	The Motivation	93
Chapter 16	The Trial Begins	97
Chapter 17	The Prosecution	101
Chapter 18	Convincing the Jury	107
Chapter 19	Meeting the Agents	113
Chapter 20	The DA Continues	117
Chapter 21	The Defense	125
Chapter 22	The Trinity	129
Chapter 23	The Technology	139

CHAPTER 1
THE GENERAL

JASON SAVAGE SAT home at his desk. The monitor focused and then there was a flash and a snapping noise. *I need to come up with a filter to stop this frequency overlap,* Jason thought. *The universal frequency seems to be rolling back on itself.*

The sound of birds singing came through the speakers. The monitor showed a window. Jason recognized this as the front right window of the cabin. (*Flash ... snap.*) *The tree is not in the right place. The others are not there.* (*Flash ... snap.*) He adjusted the input on the location-finder code. The display shifted to the left. *Excellent! I have to write this into a control.* This new system he was developing had shown flashes of promise.

Jason kept adjusting the code. The second window came into view. (*Flash ... snap.*) It was late spring. *I'm psyched.*

This lets us go all the way back to 1783. He had picked 1783 randomly, and it was the farthest back (*flash ... snap*) he had tried to view. "Man, how do I clean up this interference?" Jason asked aloud.

The voice of a woman reminded Jason of the wonder on his screen. "Thanks for [*flash ... snap*] coming over. I have to tell you about his visit."

Jason's display redirection brought two young women sitting at a table into view (*flash ... snap*). Each wore plain linen dresses. One was blueberry colored, and the other was a mustard color. The dresses stretched from their necks to the floor. Both were drawn in at the waist by woven belts. They were clearly middling women. (*Flash ... snap.*) Neither the sink nor the built-in cupboards were where they were supposed to be. Next to the handmade wooden table stood a churn, its dasher coming up and out at a slight angle. The only other (*flash ... snap*) furniture were two freestanding cupboards painted blue. The conversation continued.

"He just left a few minutes ago. He [*flash ... snap*] is wonderful. The General is so strong! He is really [*flash ... snap*] tall. He told me I am beautiful."

"Did anything [*flash ... snap*] happen between the two of you?" the other woman asked.

"No. [*Flash ... snap.*] He was such a gentleman. He did tell [*flash ... snap*] me to call him George after I called him General." (*Flash ... snap.*)

"What did he want to tell you?"

"He said he stopped by to [*flash ... snap*] tell me what a

hero my father was. He said men who [*flash ... snap*] sacrifice, like my father, were the reasons our country was now [*flash ... snap*] free."

Jason's mind almost exploded. *I must be dreaming. How many tall generals named George were around in 1783 talking about freedom?*

Jason left all the location settings as they were and reduced the intensity as minutely as he could. Typically, .0001 subtracted from the execution command set the timing back about an hour. The monitor focused. There, sitting at the table with the young woman was a man. His profile was unmistakable.

There sat General George Washington, not in uniform but breathing. *I am the first person to see a living George Washington in centuries,* thought Jason. He resembled the drawings and paintings. His eyes were striking. But his chin was weaker than most of the paintings and drawings he had seen.

"General, it [*flash ... snap*] is such a pleasure to see you!"

"The pleasure [*flash ... snap*] is all mine."

Jason thought, *This interference makes it really hard to follow.*

The young woman in the blueberry dressed continued. "The constable said you would be coming [*flash ... snap*] to town. When he told me you wanted to see [*flash ... snap*] me, I was shocked. I am so honored. Why have you come to visit [*flash ... snap*] me, sir?

Jason studied the historic legend for the next twenty-two

minutes, until the general left the cabin and the door shut behind him. (*Snap ... flash.*) "Man, how do I clean up the interference?" he complained again. Jason shut the system down and sat in silence. *How do I verify this is actual history and not some computer-generated facsimile?"* he wondered.

The next morning, Jason continued to meditate on his discoveries and the problems with the viewing interference. *Even if I figure what is wrong with the feed, who is going to believe it is real? Sure, it looks real, but computer graphics artists can do this in their sleep. How do* I *know it is real?*

Jason continued working on his technology. The technology allowed him to look back in time on actual events. He discovered the video aspect of the signals when he was fooling around with background noise. He found it was powered by electricity in the air. He made some substantial improvements due to exciting discoveries dealing with where the data was stored and nature of the electricity powering the data stream.

Then something happened that rarely happened in Kingman: a murder. The viewing had so improved that Jason thought he could possibly help law enforcement in gathering evidence. *I wonder if I can help the police solve this murder.*

Twelve months would not pass before Jason would wonder why he had pursued the system at all.

CHAPTER 2
THE MURDER

IT WAS EARLY October, and Adam was driving home from a date with a ninth-grade science teacher. She lived in the neighboring town of Mitermill. That evening he let her know how he felt about her. "I really enjoyed our time tonight. I wonder if we might have a long-term relationship. I hope so."

"I hope so too, Adam," she replied as she got out of the car.

After walking her to her door, Adam pulled away. He drove the twenty minutes back to Kingman. Billy Joel was on Adam's stereo, and he sang along, "Play us a song …" Then suddenly, out of the corner of his eye, Adam caught a glimpse of something running into the street.

"Oh my God!" A chill shot up his legs. "Where did she come from?" he asked himself aloud. He turned the car away from her. *Thump!* She ran into the side of his car. *Ohhh, I hit her!* Mashing on the brakes, Adam's car slid and ended up against the gutter. He wrestled the car door open.

Where did she come from? How? Adam was struck with an upset stomach. He reached to pick up the phone in his trembling hands and glanced at the woman. "Please be okay," he spoke quietly.

His phone slipped through his hand and clattered into the gutter. Adam scrambled to get it, but it slid again and crashed on the concrete. Finally, he picked it up only to drop it again and crack the screen. "Seriously?" Adam took a deep breath and forced his fingers to dial 911 and press send.

When the 911 operator asked, "What is your emergency?" Adam answered, "I am out here near Kingman College. I think I just hit somebody."

"What do you mean 'you think' you just hit somebody?"

"She ran into my car. I tried to miss her. She is lying in the middle of the road."

"Is she hurt?"

"I don't know. She is lying facedown."

"Don't move her. Is she breathing?"

"Yes. She is crying."

"The sheriff is on his way. I will dispatch an ambulance. They will be there shortly."

"Okay," Adam answered as he cautiously knelt over her. When she started to get up, he told her, "Don't move."

She rolled to her side. The fronts of her sweatshirt and shorts were covered with blood. He thought it was her blood, so he again said, "Don't move!"

She curled further into the fetal position there on the pavement. Adam began searching her body for the damage. Her arms and legs, at least the side he could see, appeared to be uninjured. Adam lifted and looked under her yellow sweatshirt, and in the limited light from a nearby streetlight, there appeared only smooth, soft skin. Her back, stomach, and chest were not bleeding. He could see that the bloodstains on her shorts showed the line covered by the sweatshirt and determined that the blood was from an external source.

"Are you hurt?" She shook her head. *What should I do?* he wondered. *Do I leave her lying in the street? It's wet. I can't leave her here. What do I do?* For no reason other than he thought he may have hurt her, Adam bent over and picked her up. He did not consider what the blood would do to the clothes he was wearing.

Carrying her to his car, which was still leaning into the gutter, Adam laid her in the back seat and looked around. There was a house up the long drive from which she had run. It appeared to be a multi-unit arrangement. This type of housing was typical in a college town like Kingman, New York. In the drive and surrounding yard were several cars, about six of them. One was an older black and red Corvette. This car would be a crucial piece of evidence in finding the perpetrators of the crime. As it turned out, the sheriff had gotten a call on a stolen Corvette earlier.

Adam looked around as he started to get into his car. *I wonder what caused her to run in front of me. I am so happy she is not hurt worse.* There was nothing except the loud rambling scream of an electric guitar blaring out one of the house's windows. Lights from several of the windows shone brightly. One of the side doors stood wide open. *That's strange. It is cold and clammy. I would expect all the doors and windows to be closed.* He bent in and checked on the young woman. "Are you okay?" he asked again. She nodded, sobbing and biting back screams.

Adam talked with her while he waited for the sheriff to arrive. She did not speak, so he decided to get into the car and tell her who he was. "My name is Barnes, Adam Barnes. I just moved here from Tennessee, last year. I lived in Cookeville, Tennessee, for seven years. I am originally from the lower Hudson Valley, not far from West Point. I opened that furniture store down on Main. You know the one; it used to be Haverson's Hardware Store. Susan Haverson is my salesperson. She seems to know how the residents of Kingman think. She does well with the tourists too. I make most of the stuff we sell there, mostly oak and maple furniture. I really like this town. It is so pretty and quiet and peaceful. I am hoping the store continues to do well here. I can see myself living here forever."

Just then the sheriff's car pulled up. As the sheriff and his deputy approached the driver's side, Adam rolled down the window.

"Hello, sir. My name is Sam Michaels. I am the sheriff of this county."

There was no need for an introduction. It was election season, and Sheriff Michaels's posters were everywhere. "I am Adam Barnes. I have seen your picture all around town."

"What happened here?"

"I really don't know." Adam pointed to the girl in the back seat. "I hit her. She came out of nowhere. I could not miss her. She ran into the side of my car." He pointed at the driver's side front fender. "She was covered with blood. Not from injury. From what, I don't know. She has not spoken since she ran down the driveway."

The sheriff turned, looked at his deputy, and then pointed at his eye. The deputy nodded, pulled his weapon, and started scanning the area.

Sam looked in the window, to the back seat, and nodded at the sobbing woman. She stared back at him. The sheriff took a quick look around. He said, "That's strange, the open door. "There's the 'Vette we have been looking for. We have to check out the area. It looks as if that house is a good place to start," Sam said. "Will you stay with her?" Adam got back in and sat on the front seat. His traumatized passenger was still in the back.

The sheriff and deputy went toward the house. The sheriff drew his pistol as they walked to the corvette. After looking it over, they nodded at each other and continued to the house. They approached the open door with apparent caution. Positioning themselves on opposite sides of the open, just as they do on television, Sam was first in, low with both hands holding the 9mm weapon. The deputy followed in the same manner. Through the open door, Adam saw them perform the same procedure as they entered another room further inside the apartment. He then could not see them for some time.

Other students who lived in the building started coming outside. The blaring music also stopped. Several minutes later, Sheriff Michaels and the deputy emerged. The deputy was on his handheld police radio. The sheriff walked out, scanning the entire area for what must be the perpetrator of, what Adam imagined to be, a horrible crime. After some time, the sheriff walked toward Adam's car. Opening the back door, he got in on the opposite side from the young lady. "Hello miss. My name is Sam. Are you okay?"

She did not answer. She looked up and kept crying. Her eyes were glassy with tears, and her face was contorted in anguish.

"I looked her over when I found her," Adam said. "She doesn't appear to be seriously injured."

"That's good to hear," Sam responded and turned back to her. "Can I get you to answer some questions for me?" He was at the young woman's side and took her hand. She nodded, and Sam asked in a compassionate and tender voice, "What is your name?"

"Marti Lawford."

"Were you there during the attack?" She nodded. "Do you know the name of the young woman who was attacked there in the apartment?" She nodded again. "What is her name?"

"Amber," she whimpered, "Amber Austin."

"Is she from around here?" Marti nodded. "Is she part of the Austin clan from over in Winston County?" The nod came again. "Was it a man who hurt her?" he asked softly.

"Yes … and a woman."

"And a woman?" Marti nodded.

"Now it is very important that you tell me what this man and woman looked like, what they had on, what happened, and anything they said." There was no response from Marti. "Then tell me what you can."

Adam thought, *It was very interesting how he handled such a distraught young woman.*

The sheriff calmly waited, and then Marti replied, "We … we," she whimpered, "were just talking …talking about climbing Mt. Marcy and guys. Amber … she was telling me about a new guy she had met. She was standing there holding her hand up to show me how tall he was. Then, then a rock came through the window and hit her on the arm." Adam looked toward the front porch and saw the upper window to the right of the door had a hole in it."

Marti continued, "Amber screamed and ran to the back of the living room. She was screaming, 'What happened? What happened?' Then he came through the fr … front door." She could not continue. She made a little sound and heaved with trauma.

"Go ahead, Miss," the sheriff said.

She took a deep breath and went on. "We should have had it locked …" Marti sobbed loudly.

"Go ahead," the sheriff said.

"Okay! Amber was yelling now, 'What are you doing? Why did you throw that rock?' It was like she knew him. Then *she* walked in, knocked some stuff off the wall, and said, 'Get it over with!'"

"Who walked in?" asked the sheriff.

"The girl."

"Okay, go on."

"He raised his hand. In his hand," Marti's voice climbing to a scream, "he had a knife … a big knife. And he, he …"

Marti broke down. The sheriff let her cry for a time assuring her, "We will get him. You are safe. I won't let him near you."

She looked up with glassy eyes as if to say, "I trust you." Then she started talking again. "He, he … he … hit her in the chest. The knife went, went all the way in. She screamed! She ran toward me. She hugged me and went limp."

Marti could no longer speak, and the sheriff put his arm around her. Adam had a stupid thought, *This guy has my vote.*

She curled into him and cried. Sam just hugged her, and Adam saw a tear roll out of his eye and off his cheek. The deputy came over to the window and spoke through the opening to the sheriff. "I called the ambulance, Bob [Adam found out later he was another deputy], and the fire volunteers. I will get them all sworn in as deputies. Do we know who we are looking for?"

The sheriff held a finger toward the sky to tell the deputy to wait a minute. Then he put his chin to his chest to look down at Marti. "Can you tell me who they are and what they looked like?"

Lifting her face to look at his, she spoke to the sheriff through a sharply downturned mouth. "I don't know who they are. He was tall, blond hair. He looked like a jock. He was wearing jeans and, I think, a green sweater. His eyes were so scary. They were dark."

Sam asked, "What did she look like?"

"She was beautiful. She was tall. When she was screaming, I was thinking she has such high cheekbones. Her hair was long, blonde, and straight. She had on tight jeans and a blue and gold jersey."

Marti had almost stopped crying in her effort to be accurate. The deputy had written the descriptions on a pad of paper.

"You did very well, Marti," Sheriff Michaels said. "That gives us a lot of what we need. By the way, how did you get out of there?"

She teared up and spoke through her tears, "When Amber fell?" Marti looked at him to see if he understood her. He nodded. "I looked at the guy with the knife. He started around the back of the couch toward me! I ran toward the door, and she was in my way, so I grabbed the phone and hit her with it. She fell down, and I ran by her—"

"Where did you hit her?" the sheriff interrupted.

"I, ah, think I hit her in the face."

"And then you ran where?"

"I ran and fell right there in the road. I ran into a car." Marti tipped her head toward Adam.

"That was you, sir?"

"Yes, Sheriff."

"Will you be available for questions?"

"Yes I will."

"Would you be able to stay with her until we can get her parents here?"

Marti started crying again.

"What is it, Miss?"

"My mom and dad were killed in a car accident last year." Marti broke down, crying again.

"Who shall we call then?" the sheriff asked.

"I don't know, um …"

"I will stay with her for now," Adam volunteered.

"Good," Sheriff Michaels said before getting out of the car and walking away.

The ambulance pulled up with no siren but its lights flashing. The sheriff pointed to Adam's car. Adam watched in his mirror as the flashing unit pulled behind the car. Two men jumped out of the ambulance, retrieved the gurney, and hurried to the car. Adam got out and said, "I bet you are looking for the young woman who was hit by a car."

"Yes, sir. Is the victim conscious?"

"Yes, she is conscious. She is in the back seat. She has been quite traumatized."

"Okay." One of the paramedics opened the back door and looked inside. He reached toward Marti. She withdrew. "It's okay, Miss," he said, softly.

Marti looked toward Adam as if to ask, "Is he okay?" Adam answered her questioning look. "He is okay. They need to look at you." Marti seemed to ease.

Over the next fifteen minutes they examined Marti to

assess her level of injury, if any. Finally, they exited the car, lowered the gurney, and wheeled it to the back car door.

"Come with me, Miss," the first paramedic instructed. Marti curled away from him and shook her head. "It's okay, Miss. We need to take you to the hospital. You had quite an impact."

"I didn't realize she was badly hurt," Adam stated.

"Yes, she took quite a hit. She needs to be checked out at the hospital." The paramedic reached a welcoming hand toward Marti, but she curled back again and shook her head more vigorously.

Adam tried to encourage her. "They say you need to be checked at the hospital. You need to go with them."

"No!" Marti replied firmly.

"Please go with them," Adam pled. "We need to make sure you are okay."

"No!"

"Well fellas, she doesn't want to go with you. What if I follow you to the hospital?" Turning to Marti, "Will that work for you?" Marti nodded. "Okay then, I will just follow you guys."

The first paramedic nodded. "We will take it slow. Stay right behind me."

"Okay, I will."

Adam got into his car and started it. He asked Marti if she would like to ride in the front seat. She nodded. *I bet she is afraid to get out of the car by herself,* he thought. "I will come around and get the door for you." Adam walked around to the other side of the car and helped her to the front seat. She was still shivering from the trauma of the events or the cold. Maybe a bit of both. Adam wrapped her in the blanket he kept in his car.

It took them about ten minutes to drive to the hospital. Adam filled the air with talk in an effort to keep Marti's mind off the horrible events of the night. "This was a funny way to meet someone. I am very happy to meet you. Sheriff Michaels is a great guy. You will have to come visit my store. Have you ever been to Oklahoma? I love Thanksgiving—it's the turkey and the mashed potatoes and the gravy."

They went straight to the emergency room. The deputy had already called ahead, and the staff there took them right in. Marti held tightly on to Adam's hand. He guessed she wanted him to stay close by her. He stayed right there, only looking away to afford her the privacy when they removed her blood-stained clothing. She held his hand tightly even as the doctor examined her.

The doctor asked her about a large bruise on the top of her hipbone and others that went all the way up her side to just under her arm. Marti said she did not remember when that had happened and that it all really hurt.

I don't remember seeing bruises, Adam thought. *They must be on the side that was down next to the road. That must be how I missed them.*

After a thorough exam, Marti went to radiology. The doctor thought that the impact causing the bruises might have caused internal hemorrhaging. He also found a clean cut on the inside of her wrist and thought it may be significant to the investigation. He photographed the wound. The radiologist also took several X-rays of Marti's left side. After the film was developed, the doctors discovered there had been internal bleeding and that she should rest in the hospital for the evening. At the news, Marti cried.

"I promise I will stay with you," Adam said.

At that, she hugged him and asked him to get her a second hospital gown. He got one from the nurse, and she put it on in the opposite direction from the first, thereby making sure both her front and back were covered. Marti was admitted and placed in a private room on the third floor.

After a few minutes, there was a knock on the door of the room. Adam opened the door to find Deputy Sanders standing there. He whispered so Marti could not hear, "The sheriff is worried that the assailant or assailants may still be in the area. He is afraid that because Marti is the only witness, they may try to get to her. He asked me to stand guard outside Marti's room for the night."

Sheriff Michaels had gone back to the apartment. He asked Deputy Christy to tape off the area with the yellow, "Police Line—Do Not Cross," tape. Residents not involved in the incident had gathered around the porch. The deputy had closed the curtains in the murder room and the front door. The sheriff walked up to the broken window. He made a motion, as if he throwing something through the break.

"Christy, did you call the state police coroner?"

"Yes sir. They should be here in twenty minutes."

"Thanks, Luke. I hope they don't keep us waiting."

Forty-five minutes later, the coroner's SUV pulled up the driveway. Sheriff Michaels met the vehicle at the top of the drive, near the house. Three hours later, the two people from the coroner's office came out the front door with their gurney. Amber's body laid on it in a body bag.

Sheriff Michaels got into his car. As he pulled away from the crime scene, he thought, *I can probably get a couple hours of sleep.*

In the morning, a nurse came and took Marti to get another CAT scan. When the doctor came in to look at Marti's side and listen to her left lung, abdomen, and heart, he told Marti and Adam, "The scan shows the bleeding appears to have stopped. I think it will be okay for you to go home in a while. I want you to take it very easy for the next week or so."

He took her temperature and asked her how she felt. "I am feeling sore but okay." The doctor thought the bruising on her side was from one blow. He pointed to the point on her ribs where he estimated the impact happened. It was about five inches under her arm. He told her, "Your lungs, heart, and possibly your kidneys have been damaged. Be careful." With that said, he arranged for her to go home.

When Adam and Marti were finished with the doctor, Deputy Christy stepped in to talk. "The sheriff asked me to work something out with you."

"What is it, Deputy?" Adam asked.

"He said he did not want Marti staying at her apartment alone."

"Okay. She can stay at my place. I have a guest room and bath."

"That is what I was hoping you would say."

As Deputy Christy walked them to Adam's car, he added, "The sheriff told me to tell you not to talk to anyone or tell anyone anything."

"Okay," they both responded.

"No one, but those involved in the incident know Ms. Lawford is involved at this point," the deputy explained. "The boss wants to keep this quiet. He told all of the hospital staff and doctors not to say anything about Ms. Lawford."

"Okay," they again replied.

"Go home and remain there. We will call you when we have information or instructions for you."

"All right," Adam said. "We will be waiting. Do you know when you will catch the killers?"

"No sir. We cannot promise anything right now. Just be patient; we will do our best. This type of thing doesn't happen very often around here."

The Sheriff had Adam's car parked in one of the ambulance bays. The deputy stayed with them until they were exiting the hospital drive. He said to call 911 if they had any problems.

CHAPTER 3
GOING HOME

AS HE DROVE out of the parking lot, Adam thought, *What have I gotten myself into. I am taking care of this young woman I don't even know. The police are involved. She is coming to my house. There are killers out there.* He looked over at Marti. *She is quite sweet. She has no one. It is the least I can do.* Trying to convince himself did not work. He kept coming back to, *There are killers out there.*

Adam did not see the car start following them as they pulled out of the hospital parking lot. They were only a couple of blocks on their way when Marti screamed, whirled away from the window, and curled down into the seat.

"What? What is it?"

There in a car very close to them, a man shielded the view of his face with a hand. *The killer! He has found us!* Adam's mind screamed. Grabbing his cell, Adam jammed down the gas pedal. The car lurched forward. He raised his phone to make a call. The killer's car broke off, making a fast right turn.

Adam called 911, and the operator answered quickly. The operator said he would patch Adam through to the Sheriff's cell phone. In a few seconds, he heard the operator come back on. "Go ahead, Sheriff. I have Mr. Barnes on the line."

"Hello. Mr. Barnes?"

"Yes, I'm here," Adam shouted.

"What is it?"

"I think we just saw the killer. He was waiting for us at the hospital."

"Are you in any danger?"

"I don't know! He seemed to recognized Marti. He was driving next to us for a while. I think he wanted to get to Marti or at least know where she was going. He may still be following us. I am scared."

"Okay, give me the details," Sam instructed.

"It was a green Chevy, pretty new."

"Did you get the license plate number?"

"No sorry. I didn't think to look."

"Go on."

"He drove up beside my car, and Marti saw him. She screamed. When I looked over, he had his face covered with his hand. I grabbed the cell phone, and he turned away."

"Where did he turn?"

"Right by Sweeny's Cleaners."

"I'm two blocks away. Don't go home right now. Drive

slowly to the west. I will be behind you in a few seconds." The conversation ended.

Adam looked at Marti. She was curled on the floor, weeping. She pulled the green sweatshirt; the deputy gave her over her head. She sat there, the new matching green sweatpants directly contacting the dirty floor mat. She was back to the state of shock of last night. It was completely understandable to Adam. She had looked, again into the face of the murderer. Then he noticed she had hold of his leg just below the knee. Adam reached down to touch her head. She clutched closer.

"He's gone now," Adam said. "The sheriff said he was close and would be here in a few seconds. We will talk to him soon. Sheriff Michaels will protect you." Adam spoke with all the confidence he could muster.

Within ten seconds, the sheriff's car was on Adam's back bumper. He was motioning Adam to pull over to the curb, which he did. Michaels got out of his cruiser before Adam got out of the car and was searching in all directions. "Are you okay, Mr. Barnes?"

"Please call me Adam."

"Are you all right, Adam?"

"Yes I am. I'm not so sure about Marti though."

The sheriff was still craning his neck around, looking for the killer. "Adam, go ahead and get back in the car. I have a plan."

Adam got back in the driver's side. The sheriff went around

to Marti's door and leaned in the window. "Are you okay, Marti?"

She looked up and with glassy eyes nodded. By then, one of the deputies had arrived. As the man walked up to the car, Sheriff Michaels stood up and spoke softly to his assistant. The deputy began visual sweeps of the entire scene. Michaels leaned back into the car. "In order to have a more secure place for you to stay, we need to be sure we have lost this guy who has been following you."

"Okay," Adam said.

"Here's what I want you to do. Take Main Street here straight on out of town, over the bridge at Crazy Creek, on up to Nolan Road. Take a left up the hill at Nolan Road. Follow it up two miles and go right on Underwood. Take Underwood all the way back down across Highway 26 and back up through to your house. I will wait on Nolan to see if he is behind you. I will have Christy here wait just beyond Highway 26 for a second check. Go up to your place. Do not come out until I tell you. If you need anything, call me. I will see that you get it. All right?" Adam nodded. "Okay, wait for me to pull away. I will have Christy trail you at a distance until you turn at Nolan. I'll talk to you later." The sheriff walked back to his car.

They drove through the sheriff's plan, and it seemed to work well. When they came to the end, Michaels pulled over and got out of his car. "According to Christy, no one was following us. Go home. Stay there. If you need anything, call me. We will bring it to you."

"Okay," Adam answered.

"I will have a deputy in your driveway."

CHAPTER
— 4 —
THE NEXT DAY

THE NEXT MORNING, Adam awakened, showered, and was downstairs when the newspaper arrived. He had not slept well. What surprised him was how well Marti seemed to have slept. He presumed she was subconsciously escaping the horrible waking hours of yesterday. The thump of the newspaper hitting the porch made him jump. He walked to the door, opened it, and retrieved the *Kingman Gazette*.

The front page was as he expected. Plastered across the top were the words, "Kingman Coed Killed." Below the headline was her picture. Amber Austin was a cute girl. She was not pretty or beautiful. She had one of those terribly appealing qualities that he was confident allowed her no shortage of dates. Amber's hair was a chestnut color. Her eyes were brown.

She had a wonderful smile. The caption simply read, "Kingman College coed Amber Austin."

He began to read the news. The reporter wrote some of the details of the crime. Some were not even close to being right. He wondered if the sheriff had purposely fed the reporter some misinformation. She also wrote about Amber's background and family. She stated that Amber was studying elementary education. Near the end of the article, the following line caught his eye and imagination:

> Sheriff Michaels is being assisted in the investigation by Kingman College professor Jason Savage.

Most of what Adam knew about Professor Savage he read in the *Gazette*. It seemed he was newsworthy for the shock value. Adam read on.

Who Is Jason Savage?

Jason Savage came to Kingman College about a year and a half ago. The head of the college science department, Dr. Mark Burns, called Savage when Dr. Everett Browstein fell down the stairs outside the computer lab. Unfortunately, Dr. Browstein did not survive the fall.

Burns lobbied the stodgy decision-makers of Kingman College to take a look at Savage. They originally balked at hiring him. Dr. Burns eventually won them over, and Dr. Savage was offered a position.

He was only nineteen years of age. He finished his master's in computer science from Rensselaer Polytech the age of sixteen and his doctorate from MIT at nineteen. Savage had been unemployed (working on his own research) until Kingman hired him. No one else inquired about the position, even though it was advertised on all job board sites. He took the job even though Kingman does not have a very good reputation in the computer world.

Savage thought it might work out to be a good fit, saying, "No one will question my research."

Not only had Savage achieved substantial professional degrees, he also owned a fierce perspective of independence. He did not adhere to Kingman's accepted attire or grooming guidelines.

Dr. Savage has red hair that is extremely thick and long. Its length was a major sticking point for the head of the department. The faculty and students have gotten used to his youthful look, attire, and independent attitude. He is a genius, having won national attention for his postgraduate innovation in computer sciences and technology.

Savage suffered difficulty securing a place to live when he came to town. He originally found someone to rent him a room. That, however, lasted only three weeks. He ended up in an ancient cabin out by Lake Teardrop. There were rumors this place had been standing since the 1700s. Jason was quoted as saying, "I am so happy to be teaching at the college. I do wish they had hardware that is more capable in the computer lab. That stuff will hardly run word processing software. Well I can at least build a top-of-the-line setup here in my little stone castle by the lake."

The discrimination of the faculty passed quickly as Savage was recognized as a genius for his innovations in the world of computer science. He discovered a way to store three times the data on a standard hard drive. This simple discovery brought great rewards to the college. That was the reason for his title—professor—in his early twenties. The institution's department heads were afraid of criticism if they were to leave his title as "Instructor Jason Savage."

Adam admired a picture of Savage at last year's graduation. He looked rather unique in his commencement attire. You know, the puffy-type headwear and robes worn by those who have earned doctorates. His long red hair added to his persona.

He had come into Adam's store about a month ago. Jason asked if Adam could make him a custom computer desk. "Sure," Adam said, "but why don't you take a look at some of my custom designs?"

Jason handed Adam a drawing he'd made using one of his computers. None of Adam's designs would have worked for the doctor's arrangement. He made Jason a desk in oak and walnut. His specifications were precise. Adam had to admit one of the features—the mouse pad shelf—was ingenious, being closer in, slightly turned inward, and a little lower than the keyboard. It was quite comfortable and took a little less elbow twist to operate. Adam had thought, *This kid is a thinker.*

Putting the newspaper down, Adam decided to check on Marti. Walking to the stairs, he pondered how Savage could be aiding the investigation, and why the sheriff would want someone to know about his involvement. As he opened her door, he saw Marti, lying on her side under the sheet and quilt. Her brown hair, nicely highlighted and slightly shorter than shoulder length, rested over her face. Her face, which he could see through the brunette layer, looked like that of an angel. He could not see her clear brown eyes. They were closed. Her perfect little nose made a nice silhouette against the pillow. She looked so peaceful. He was glad and at the same, time, amazed she had, actually, been able to sleep.

The floor creaked where he stood, and Marti's eyes opened. Within a second, they grew wide. She obviously remembered recent history. She gasped. He moved over and spoke before touching her so not to scare her. "Good morning, Marti. How did you sleep?"

She did not speak. Her eyes still stared straight ahead.

"The sun is up, and it is getting quite warm out. Maybe we can go for a walk in a while." That might have been a stupid thing to say, but at the time, he was looking for anything. Adam grew uneasy and decided to leave. "I will be down in the kitche—"

"Auhhh!" she cried out. Marti grabbed his hand. Her grip surprised him.

"Do you want me to stay?" She nodded.

Adam sat on the edge of the bed. Marti did not seem to be able to move. She was trembling again. "Do you need to use the bathroom?"

She nodded, so he helped her to her feet and led her to the door. He stopped at the doorway; she stopped and would not go in. Adam said, "I can't go in there with you."

She shrugged in concession, released his hand, and went inside. She pushed the door closed, stopping it short of latching. He got the message. Marti finished and began to run water in the shower. Adam looked away from the door and slumped against the wall. Just then, her hand reached through the narrow opening in the doorway and closed around his arm. As he turned, he saw that Marti was not wearing any clothes and had covered herself with a towel. He tried not to look anywhere except her face. She pushed open the door and pulled him inside.

I don't think this is such a good idea, Adam thought. But he could tell she needed him close to feel comfortable. She stepped behind the opaque shower curtain and threw the towel over the curtain rod.

He turned away to give her privacy. Adam heard her step under the shower. He then realized, he was staring into a mirror, which through a gap in the end of the shower curtain gave him a perfect reflection.

I should not look. What the heck? I can't help it.

He saw a complete profile of Marti's body, the side without the bruises. She was beautiful. Marti had a small athletic build. Her muscular body looked to be quite strong. Her round bottom was perfect. Her small shapely breasts were nothing less than … He did his best to forget the beautiful young woman.

After her shower, Marti dried and wrapped herself in the terrycloth robe Adam had hanging on the back of the door. She took hold of his hand, and he led her down to the kitchen. He fixed her pancakes and a cup of tea. Adam made himself tea, too, and sat down with her. He picked up the paper and began reading to himself while she ate.

> Professor Savage was recently recognized for his new solid memory retrieval software (maximizing read only memory [ROM] storage).

Professor Savage is twenty-two years old and is a native of Carthage, Missouri. Savage joined the faculty of the Kingman College, October a year and a half ago, after the unexpected death of Dr. Everett Browstein.

Savage told us he brings a new technology to bear in this investigation. This, his latest innovation, uses a proprietary technology he calls the Universal Computer (UC). Savage told us, "Using UC, we will be able to gather evidence the likes of which has never before existed." The professor appeared quite excited when he told us about being contacted by Sheriff Michaels.

When asked, Sheriff Michaels told the *Gazette*,

"As of now, the UC process is not admissible in court.' In this reporter's opinion, based on Savages' claims, this new development will completely revolutionize evidence-gathering procedures at a crime scene.

CHAPTER 5
THE PARK

SHORTLY AFTER BREAKFAST, the sheriff brought a supply of the clothes and shoes he thought appropriate from Marti's room at the apartment. "You two should find some way to relax," the sheriff suggested.

Adam thought, *I think it makes sense to get Marti out of the house.* "Marti, let's take a walk in the park."

"Sure!"

"Why don't you wear those hiking boots. I think they are best for the terrain we will be walking."

"Sounds good."

They wore jeans as the temperature was not one to warrant shorts. Shorts would also subject a soul to scratches. Sweatshirts were also the garb of the day.

The sheriff gave his permission to journey into the

wilderness. He made them promise to "Stay away from the roads. I mean, don't be seen, and be very aware if you were being followed." Adam's repeated assurances eased Michael's concerns enough to let them walk in the woods. The sheriff gave Adam a radio. "Carry this all the time."

"I promise to carry it."

Michaels whispered. "Please do. They may be trying to get rid of a witness."

Whispering back, Adam asked, "How long do you think we will have to be careful?"

"Not sure. Hopefully we will get some leads, and we will bring them in."

"What then?"

"Well we have some really good conventional evidence, but I am really counting on Jason's technology."

"Why is that?"

"It looks back in time and can produce audio and video."

"Wow!"

"Yeah. It's a game changer. Just be careful." Adam nodded with understanding. Sam walked out the door. "See ya." He walked to his car and drove away.

In a short while, Adam and Marti walked on to the thickening grass of his backyard. Adam had a sudden thought. *This yard takes me more than two hours to mow at the heat of the summer. I would hire someone if it were not such great thinking time.*

They started into the woods and through a stand of pines that formed the boundary of the park. Within ten minutes, they were beyond sight and most of the sounds of civilization. The forest was coming alive with the finer undergrowth. The leaves were already in the tops of the trees. There was a slight breeze that caused some of the more still winter-hardened parts of the lower trees to snap together and make rather stark scraping noises as they rubbed. The weather-matted leaves, which formed most of the forest flooring, offered a muffled, muted crunching. Spring has a fresh smell to it as you near the month of May in upstate New York, and this freshness was everywhere.

Downtown Kingman was built on the level ground of an ancient, now silent, riverbed. The residential parts began on the rolling hills outside of downtown. The park began the climb of the land toward the mountains. As Adam and Marti began their trek, the walking was easy. The forest, typical of mature woods, offered good passage. The thick trunks of the coarsely barked pines sported dried, broken stubs of the early branches that once brought shape to the young trees but were no longer useful or living. These limbs had always fascinated Adam. He thought about the history and the people they may have touched. But they broke easily, and once broken to the base, are remembered no more.

Their conversation was limited as they headed deeper into the trees. Marti whispered, "Look at the cardinal." She pointed to a flaming red male, front lit, about twenty feet up in a rich green pine.

They came to the first brook. There were plenty of stones on which to step to get across, and it ran slowly. This same stream fed the small lake in the park designed for easy public access.

The wildflowers were abundant that fine spring morning. They passed several stands of wild irises. Their royal purple and bright yellow colors lent further life to the vivid green of their stalks and leaves. The gray stones even seemed alive next to these regal blossoms.

On a now unused log road they saw bluets. They formed a frostlike cover of pale blue and white beside the needle-covered paths. The moss was plentiful, often covering stumps and streambeds. It was everywhere, clinging to the north side of the trunks and eventually growing around the entire base.

Moving upward inside the park were more deciduous trees. The poplar and birch were Adam's favorites. The birch for their white bark and green leaves, the poplar for their soft popping of leaves in the breeze. For Adam, reality seemed distant while in nature. It was beautiful, and he hoped Marti was experiencing the same that morning.

Marti was a most interesting young woman. He was growing fond of her company. Though she spoke little, she had a style. Much of the wonderful scenery went by without notice as he studied her mannerisms. She moved confidently when he would have thought her to be in an extremely vulnerable state. In some ways, maybe Adam was the vulnerable one.

Their climb was vertical now. He remembered always being impressed with the altitude of this lake. The first time he had the pleasure of seeing it was a bit over a year ago. It was inspiring being so close to the sky and over six hundred feet higher than the highest streets of Kingman. He decided the reason God put the lake so high into the park was so he could make the falls. They were coming to the falls.

Marti stopped at a level spot and looked back at Adam. The sun was shining through the leaves of a towering maple. Patches of sunlight reflected off her cheek, which looked so soft, and flashed in her eyes.

"Just up there are the waterfalls," Adam said.

"Oh, let's go look."

He wanted to keep her talking, so he asked, "Have you been up here yet?"

"No."

"I think you will like this."

Ahead, the rushing of the falling water was constant and soothing. They walked around a large rock outcropping. The sun shone down on the old stone and reflected off the crystal facets in the rock. The stone was fractured in many places, and soil and grass filled the gaps. Some wildflowers Adam did not recognize added a purple accent to the scene. Then the falls came into view. Getting closer, he remembered how loud the roaring was when you were close.

If it were not for the forest, the falls would be visible for miles. Seneca Creek, the stream that fed the falls, came through the lake having originated high in the mountains. The water was cold and clear. At the top, where the water flung itself into the air, the water changed from clear to white as the air and the weightlessness made it foam. The mist at this level was heavy. In the heat of a summer day, this was good. This time of spring, it was not. Adam yelled over the rushing, "We need to move up, or we will get drenched and catch cold." Marti nodded. They walked back into the forest and wound back and forth toward the crest.

At the top of the falls, they went to a large flat rock that jutted out over the edge of the cliff. From there they were able to see the rapids above the lake and the water landing on the rocks below. This was Adam's favorite spot. He sat and Marti cuddled in close.

After a while, they walked the shore of the quarter-mile-long glacial lake. The breeze had settled as they sat on a log at the east end of the shore. The mountains to the northwest reflected off the surface of the water like a mirror. The main public area was about a third of the way up the lakeshore line, to the left. There were only a few people along the shore. Adam noticed a man about a quarter mile in that direction looking their way through binoculars. *What the hell?* Adam wondered.

The man seemed quite intent on getting a good look at them. After two or three minutes of his spying on them, Adam began to get nervous. *Oh my God! Is that the killer?* He tried not to let Marti see him checking out the spy. *I've got to call the sheriff.* Adam tried to slide out the radio, but Marti turned and smiled at him just as it was about to clear his pocket. He smiled back and slid the radio back into his pocket. *What now?*

He pretended to look over by the lake as if taking in the scenery. But the black smudge that didn't belong—a man, not too tall but wiry—was still there. Just as Marti turned to face where the man was, Adam pointed in the other direction. "A warbler! Did you see it?" Marti turned to scan the treetops.

There is no time for the sheriff. It's up to me, Adam thought.

CHAPTER
—— 6 ——
THE CRIME SCENE

SHERIFF MICHAELS STOOD in the front doorway, surveying the murder room. Beside the sofa where they had earlier removed Amber's body, surrounding the large area of blood, were sprays and spatters of stain. The patterns looked like blood spurting from a wound under pressure. *This is horrible,* he thought.

On the carpet, not far from the other end of the couch, was a shattered clock. There, too, were a couple of framed pictures, one facedown, the other face up with a broken pane of glass. It appeared to be a picture of one of their mothers.

There were footprints made by what appeared to be men's athletic shoes. They led from where Amber fell, around the sofa, and toward the door. They passed another bloodstain, smaller than the first. From this second dried pool, droplets trailed to the front door.

The county, being sparsely populated, supported only the sheriff and three deputies. Michaels had to call in the troopers. Their crime lab and morgue were in Syracuse, an hour and a half south. This situation would work but would delay their findings. The state homicide team and coroner had been there and left. They had retrieved fingerprints and taken photos and blood samples from both blood trails/stains. The troopers said they were confident in the evidence they gathered. They did say they were not confident that the database would hold matches.

The sheriff had posted notices around campus asking for the public's help. The notice asked if anyone knew something germane to the case to call the sheriff's office with that information. Some of the items listed were blood on clothing, injuries suffered, unusual obsessions, suspicious behaviors, known disagreements with the victim, and anyone having seen the Corvette that evening. No one had come forth yet.

The "Police Line" tape was still in place outside the apartment. The locks were changed, so no one would unknowingly contaminate the crime scene. The Corvette had been hauled and scoured. DNA was available in both the apartment and the car. Then the car was released to its owner. In the *Gazette*, the sheriff requested anyone having information about or had seen activity around the area where the car was stolen to call. Michaels had been told the DNA results usually took a few days to complete.

This was a typical crime scene with typical evidence, except for one thing: Jason's system.

Michaels thought it was crazy at first. Whoever heard of walls holding information, like sounds? And even if it did work—and Michaels was not yet convinced—would it hold up in court?

He sighed as Jason's car pull up. *I sure hope it works. I have seen this defense attorney pull some fast ones. What is there to lose?* Jason had introduced Sam to his system, but he had not seen it work. But he was hopeful. However, even if Jason's evidence was substantial, this type of evidence had never been seen before, let alone proven admissible. If the evidence from the professor appeared to be substantial, the sheriff thought he had an idea that might influence a favorable ruling on admissibility. *What is there to lose?* For now, he was waiting for Jason.

A couple of minutes later, Savage walked up the pavement. He was carrying a small computer bag. "Hello again, Jason!"

"Hi, Sheriff!"

"How do we do this?"

"As I told you earlier, all we have to do is put three sensors on an appropriate surface and gather the data. It should only take us a couple of minutes. Then I have to take the data back to the office, narrow down the period, and compile the report."

"Which surface can you use?"

"I think these are old plaster walls, right?"

"Yeah. Most of these old buildings still have their original plaster/lath structure in place."

"Excellent! These walls have plenty of data storage capability." The sheriff shrugged, and Savage nodded with a smile. Jason selected a wall in the front room above Amber's bloodstain. He placed his tablet on the table beside the sofa and held a polymer triangular frame to the wall. "It has three sensors on the points. They will gather the data." He held it there for about a minute.

"That should do it. Oh, one more thing." The professor lifted his tablet in the air and typed a short code into it. "This will read the background noise."

Michaels had a lot of questions to ask. How could a wall store information? What was background noise? If the plaster were an acceptable storage facilitator, why did it still work with paint on it? He decided he would hold them until it was time to convince the judge to admit the evidence. At this point, all he could do was wait.

CHAPTER

—— 7 ——

THE CHASE

JUST THEN ADAM noticed the man, spying on them, pack his binoculars away and begin to take a determined stride along the shore of the glacial lake. Fear swelled in Adam's stomach. He felt weak and numb. He commanded, "Let's go!"

Marti seemed shocked. "What?"

"Someone was looking at us across the way, there," Adam said pointing. "And he is coming our way."

Marti turned toward the approaching figure. She gasped when she recognized him and started to run.

"Let's go," Adam said. "We have a few hundred yards on him. I know these woods. If we are smart and keep a steady pace, he will not be able to keep up with us. You must listen to me. We have to stay calm."

Adam thought he had come across controlled. Nevertheless,

his actual feelings were about 150 miles from there. Marti did not speak. Adam looked at her eyes. She had that scared kid look, the look a person gets when someone jumps out of the dark at him or her. He ran, and she stayed right with him. He decided to set the pursuer off in the wrong direction. He moved quickly back into the woods in the opposite direction he knew they would actually be heading.

The air suddenly felt hot. They had not run far enough to break a sweat, yet he was already soaked. They ran up the slope away from his house and over some large rock outcroppings. There were several crystal deposits in the stone, and it sparkled as they strode across it. As they came up to tall pine trees, they grabbed the trunks and swung around them. Marti slipped on some leaves. Adam grabbed her arm and hoisted her. She whimpered. He wanted to stop to comfort her, but he knew he could not. They crested another rock outcropping. Adam turned. There, about 150 yards behind them, stood the man. *Close. Too close.*

A shot rang through the forest, ricocheting off a nearby tree trunk. An explosion sent great chunks of bark and wood quietly to the forest floor. Marti fell hard on the rock. She was gasping for air when he pulled her to her feet. "We've got to stay ahead of him and out of sight."

The gun was a variable Adam had not considered. *I have to stay calm. I have to.*

"There is a small cavern about a quarter of a mile up the slope," Adam said. "It is hard to see the entrance, especially if one is running. If we can get to that opening, he might not find us."

They approached the cave's mouth. Its opening stood behind some brush at the base of a tall rock cliff. Adam pulled back the overgrowth with his left hand. The thorns on the branches tore his arm. He barely felt the pain, but he did notice the blood. There was a lot of it. Marti stepped in and down. He followed her.

Inside the cave was cold and damp. It was like that the last time he was in there. It was very dark, and it took a minute for his eyes to adjust. He remembered how the cave wandered around. He remembered thinking this would be a great place for kids to play. But some of the passages circled around, allowing one to end up behind another. *I hope he did not see us come in here. If he did, he should be here in twenty seconds.*

Marti was hugging his arm, the one that was bleeding. He could feel the warm liquid running down his arm. Adam could hear her panting and feel her heart pounding. She was scared. He decided to prepare her. "If he saw us come in here, he should be coming in really soon." He looked at her, and even in the scant light, he could see her eyes glaring. "You've got to be quiet, okay?" Adam said, his voice echoing against the close walls. "Now stay behind me and hang on."

"You are hurt."

"Can't think about it now."

He heard the brush move outside the entrance. The pursuer said, "Shit!"

The thorns got another victim, Adam thought. "He is

coming in, Marti. We have to move." He tried to remember which way would get them out or that would, at least, put them behind him. *I have to be brave and get aggressive with this man.* He was very nervous and wondered if he could muster the nerve to do what he might be required to do.

As Adam and Marti went deeper into the earth, the darkness was blacker, and the humidity got thicker. They had to move as fast as possible, and they had to remain quiet. The pursuer could shoot into the darkness at the sound.

Adam's hands went up and down the wet rock of the cave walls. His feet tested the floor, or lack of floor. He pretended to be blind and imagine how he might move about a room without the benefit of sight. Then the palm of his hand moved across something warm and fuzzy. His eyes could not see what the object was, but his mind screamed. The bat let out a scratchy shrill and began to fly. Adam grabbed Marti and pulled her to the mud (or what he hoped was mud) of the floor. Within an instant, a shot rang out. Fragments of shattered rock made Adam tightly close his eyelids. That was when he realized that his eyes had been open even though they served no purpose in the blackness.

At the blast, thousands of winged mammals took to the air. The sound was like muffled thunder in the closeness of the cave. Adam knew this was the time to move. *It may be our only chance,* Adam thought. "Come on," Adam yelled above the rush.

They moved quickly along the slimy wall. He thought he remembered a passage to the right just ahead. They came to a corner in the wall and moved around it. As they did, Adam saw a bluish glow fill the main chamber. *He's got a cigarette lighter,* Adam thought. *If we don't stay ahead of him, we're done for.* Adam used the light to get a fix on the obstacles in the passage. He decided he needed to get around and behind the pursuer while the noise was still ongoing. He knew it would be quiet when the bats left the cave.

The tunnel curved quickly around to the right. Adam hoped the killer was trying to follow them. If not, they could not get behind him. Then he thought, *How did he find us? The sheriff's plan had not worked ... Not now!*

The rush from the bats' exit was subsiding. It grew quiet again. Very quiet. *Where is he?* Adam wondered. Just then, Adam heard, "Uuhhh," with a puff of air. *That sounded like he fell.*

The lighter lit again, and Adam instantly realized the puffing had not come from their pursuer. A large black bear headed toward the blue light. It roared as it attacked. The light dropped, and Adam heard, *Bang! Bang!*

The bear got him. Their pursuer yelled, and then it went quiet. Adam heard his moans and his scuffling to get away. The moaning of the injured man grew quieter and quieter.

Adam and Marti did not move for several minutes. Finally, Adam broke the silence. "I think we can go now. I think that bear got him good."

They finished their circling and approached the main entrance. Adam was able to make out the walls and ceiling. Closer to the opening, he saw the bear, no longer breathing.

He scanned everywhere for the gunman, but he did not see him. There was quite a bit of blood near the bear and trailing outside. Adam assumed the bear had done its damage.

He slowly crept out of the cave opening. He saw no one. Marti was crawling behind him. He said, "Let's wait awhile." Adam pulled out the radio the sheriff gave him. "I wish I had time to use this fifteen minutes ago. Hello, hello, this is Adam Barnes. Sheriff, can you hear me?"

"This is Sam. Go ahead."

"Sheriff, we have been chased and shot at. We need some help."

"Okay. Where are you?"

"We are near a cave northwest of the falls."

"Sheriff, this is Roberts."

"Go ahead, deputy."

"I know the cave, and I am in position."

"Go ahead, Bob. Go find them."

"On my way. Roberts out."

"Okay, Adam, wait there and stay alert. Deputy Roberts is on his way."

They waited and listened for some time. Adam saw someone running toward them. His first thought was that the guy was back. Then he caught a glimpse of a blue uniform. It was not the gunman. It was the deputy who had been stationed outside Adam's house. The deputy called to him. "Are you okay? I heard a shot!"

"Yes, he missed us. I think he is hurt. A bear got him inside this cave." Adam pointed. "I heard him run."

The deputy immediately grabbed his radio and squatted. "Roberts to base."

"Go ahead, Deputy."

"I am up in the park, by the lake. I have Barnes and the girl. Apparently the suspect found them. I think the suspect is hurt, possibly injured by a bear. Tell the sheriff I will escort them off the mountain and to the house. We must be careful. I don't know if the suspect is gone."

"Ten-four."

Deputy Roberts had grabbed a stretchy bandage from his vest. He slowly wrapped it around Adam's arm, trying to stop the bleeding. They slowly and cautiously headed down the trail.

CHAPTER
—— 8 ——
THE DATA IS RELIABLE

JASON SAT AT his desk, thinking about the events of the last few days. Never had he been so near to a crime and what happens after the crime. This was the first time anyone wanted to see his discovery used to gather evidence. When he first started discovering the miracle that would become an epiphany, he had no idea to where and to what extent the discovery would take him.

He was thankful that the sheriff had taken an interest in the technology. Jason told Sheriff Michaels it would revolutionize the gathering of crime scene evidence. There had been limited time to explain it to the sheriff as he had to place sensors on the walls where an event happened to get pertinent data. It seemed that every day Jason was able to work in this technology, his capabilities doubled. Now, only a couple days later, he had the ability to pull data based on GPS location and a point in time. As it turned out, the information was coming from a computer. Jason wondered, *Can I be sure the information I pull is truthful and accurate?*

Jason felt his phone vibrate. He recognized the number as that of Sheriff Sam Michaels. "Hello, Sheriff Michaels."

"I told you to call me Sam."

"Sorry, Sam. What can I do for you?"

"I want to get together so you can explain this thing to me."

"Sounds good. I also have the results from the crime scene to show you."

"Great, Jason. When should I come over?"

"How about today after class? Say four o'clock?"

"Sixteen hundred hours. I will be there. I have your address as 500 Simpson Street, the Simpson Building, suite 500. Is that right?"

Looking at his surroundings, Jason answered, "Yes sir. I am in the attic."

"See ya this afternoon."

"Cool. Bye."

"Bye."

Sheriff Michaels arrived just before four o'clock. He pulled into an open space in the parking lot in front of the Simpson Building. He went inside and climbed the steps to the fifth floor. Sam knocked on the door that had "Dr. Jason Savage" on a brass plate.

"Come on in, Sam."

On his second step, a floor board creaked. Looking further

in, he could see Jason sitting in the middle of the large attic with three, only three, walls surrounding him. There was a hint of old wood in the air of the attic office. As Sam got closer, he noticed the wall behind Jason's desk was full of diplomas. On another wall hung a guitar and three posters. One was of Jimi Hendrix, one was of Eric Clapton, and one of Jimmy Page. The sheriff recognized all of them as great rock guitarists. *I remember them all. Few kids his age appreciate them anymore.* Sam thought. "How are you, professor?" Over a chuckle he said, "I mean Jason."

"I'm good."

"Thanks for taking time to see me."

"No prob. Great to see you!"

Sam thought. *I have to say this right. I don't want to give him the impression I don't trust him.* "You know, this upcoming trial really has me nervous."

Jason looked up. "Why, Sam? You seem to have a bunch of good evidence."

"I do. There is just something. I can't put my finger on it, but I really need your system to work like you told me it would."

"It will, Sam," Jason said with as much conviction as he could. He still wasn't sure it was completely accurate. "Come on in and sit down." Sam took his seat.

"Jason, tell me about you and this system of yours."

"How far do you want me to go back?"

"If I am going to trust you, I need to know where you came from."

Jason leaned back in his chair and heard his stomach growl. He smiled. "Okay, Sam. I will go back to when I knew I would be working in the IT world. It all started when I was young. Computers were everywhere. I enjoyed games and figuring out how they worked. It was not long until I realized it was more fun to manipulate the programs than to play the games. I spent a good deal of my youth writing surprises into games.

"My dad died when I was seven. My mom, my brother, and I did not have much money, so I used the computers at school to have fun. It got to the point that I could not do what I wanted on the school computers. Since we could not afford our own, I figured out a way to get one to use.

"After school, when I was about fourteen, I used to work in a small grocery store owned by a local family. I helped them unpack and stock the shelves for an hour or so each day. Now every night when I went home, Mr. Beck—Jerome, as we called him—was hunched over the ledgers, figuring inventory, and ordering. Mrs. Beck was adding up the receipts and paying the bills. I wondered how long they were there every night. One night I asked them. They told me they were there for two and a half to three hours each night. I told them we could set up a system to do all this work in minutes. It would cost about three thousand dollars. It would consist of a scanner and two computers. They agreed to do it.

"I set up the hardware and programmed it. One of the computers I set up remotely, in my home. I was able to digitize their inventory and ordering and their receivables and payables. I told them I would monitor it each night. It only took me a half an hour to verify the data. The rest of the time I had the computer to use."

"Nice," Sam said.

"Yeah, it worked out well. So now I had the machine. Next was to narrow down the research to pursue.

My mom is very religious and always took us to church. I listened to the teachings closely and believed. When I was about eight, I remember the preacher talking about Jesus coming into Jerusalem. He called it the 'Triumphal Entry.' Something in that story really grabbed me. The religious leaders there were telling him to stop the crowd from praising him." He pointed to a frame on the wall. The writing in the frame said.

> ◀ Luke 19:39-40 ▶Some of the Pharisees in the crowd said to Him, "Teacher, rebuke your disciples." But Jesus answered, "I tell you, if these become silent, the stones will cry out!"

"Jesus's statement struck true. I still think about it much of the time. How could the rocks cry out? Were they alive? How could it be? I doubted my questioning many times, but it struck me as truth. So there I was, a geek, thinking about rocks." He stopped, shook his head, and seemed to drift off into a memory.

"Right, rocks! I started to build a laboratory and a research structure. I studied all three types of rocks. I studied whole and crushed rock. I exposed them to all types of stimuli and recorded any results. I gathered no substantial findings.

"I asked myself if Jesus really said this or if men added it. I mulled this over a hundred times. It was plain to me that no man would write this into the story. The concept is bizarre. It would only cause questions, distracting from the message. Therefore, I went into asking mode. I started asking myself questions as to what he could have meant."

"Where did that lead you?" Sam asked.

"Well, hold on." Jason stood up and walked around the end of the desk, slowly shaking his head from side to side, his great locks like a pendulum. "Let me tell you, Sam, from time to time I come to a conclusion that strikes me as a truth. I believed Jesus's statement about the rocks crying out as a truth. So I kept asking. This led me to the study of how crystals can store data. Studying solid data storage was fun, but there was an issue gnawing at me. It is reliable, but solid storage needs a constant source of power. If not, it would lose its stored data.

"Even if I solved that, what about where this data originated? And then, how was this data delivered? If I answered these, I would have to determine how the stored data was organized, and once stored and organized, how were the electrons excited to release relevant information? And on and on and on. I wondered if I would ever know.

"As you can see, Sam, I had a bunch to settle. I was listening to everything and conducting experiments for each question and subset of questions. I decided this might be a lifelong endeavor. That frustrated me.

"I thought about the process in which I was involved, based on 'feeling' or 'impression' that something was true. I made another decision, to rely on the presupposition that these feelings and/or impressions may be more. I considered the possibility these may be directed by my subconscious or something else!"

Those few minutes seemed like hours to Sam. There was so much to consider and learn. He told Jason they would have to meet again. He needed time to consider everything Jason had told him.

Two weeks later, Sam met Jason on the bench at the crest of the hill. Jason turned to look at Sam. In Jason's eyes were excitement and questions. "Sam, remember I told you about the things that I was confident were truths?"

"Yeah."

"Well, there are other things that happened that I can't explain."

"Like what?"

"One time I was working on editing an equation. I had tried several routes and options. I was ready to quit because I could not get the program to focus on the variables of the background noise. Then a thought hit me. I was focusing on strands of the universal hum. What if I could have the machine focus on the strands of data and the entire hum at the same time?"

"Wow! You mean there is more than one strand of flowing data in the background noise?" Sam asked.

"Yeah, hundreds, maybe thousands of strands! I had to

rework my formulas and code. That took me months to set up. Once I did it, I programmed my machine to focus on a strand of data. I realized during the refitting process that the strand of data was not on a common frequency wave, so I could not try to read it like a regular wave. It was powered by static electricity, so I had to let it read from a stationary point in the wave. The interference cleared. You see, it was not interference; it was more information. Suddenly it was all open to me."

"Oh my."

"Yeah! Then I tried to do some searches. I could not get results. It seemed the amount of data available was overwhelming my system. I multiplied the RAM and the same results. I worked on that one for months too. Then an epiphany!"

"Keep going!"

"Okay, so I was working with this omnipresent system with so much power and information, and I can't search it. Without a search capability, I could only pick dates and times to explore. How limited is that? Then the epiphany! What if it had its own search feature?

"When I would sit and work in the program, I could watch real history, or at least I assumed it was real. It made sense to me that the only way I could be sure it was real and reliable was to test it on myself. Thinking about an event only I would know about, I typed a location—'Cobleskill, NY 9/25/2015 8:30 p.m., Shinapole Campground—Savage under picnic table.' The monitor flashed to life. There before me was an image of me at fourteen. I had just gotten out from under the table. I spoke out, 'Oh just ten minutes earlier.' The search automatically updated by my voice command.

"There I was, milling around with fellow teens. The game we were playing was trying to fit as many of us into various spaces. Someone said, 'Let's try under the picnic table,' and we started to pile under the table. I spoke, 'Change the perspective five feet to the left.' As if the cameraperson had moved to the left, my view changed. I watched carefully as I snugged in next to Beverly Holder. As we squeezed together, I saw my hand reach up in front of her breast. We pressed together, and I knew she wouldn't differentiate my hand from all the other crushing. I can still feel her heart beating through that handful. Beverly didn't even know. I was the only one ... It was real. It is reliable. Now I have to make other people believe."

Jason saw the astonished look on Sam's face. "Too much?"

"Yeah. It is a lot to think about."

"Okay. Enough for tonight."

Jason pulled open a drawer on his desk and pulled out a CD. "Here is what is important right now. Take this with you, and watch it when you are ready."

CHAPTER 9
THE KILLER'S MISTAKE

DEPUTY LUKE CHRISTY was only four years from retiring. He had been with the county for thirty-three years. He was Sheriff Michael's right-hand man. An imposing figure, he stood about six feet two inches with a solid frame and mannerism. He wore glasses.

After Deputy Roberts reported the killer had been injured by a bear, Deputy Luke had taken it upon himself to alert all the surrounding counties to be on the lookout for injuries that could have been caused by a bear. Three days after Roberts escorted Sam and Marti from the park, Herimer County Regional Hospital called the sheriff's office and asked for Deputy Luke.

"Hello, this is Luke Christy."

"Yes, Deputy Christy, this is chief nurse Hanifa Gobar calling from the Herimer County Regional Hospital."

"How may I help you, Nurse Gobar?"

"Deputy, we have a fellow here who has injuries that look like bear claw lacerations. The injuries look to be several days old. The patient apparently tried to treat them himself, but they are infected now. Do you want us to call the sheriff and have him hold this fellow?"

"Please call the sheriff and have him take a look at this fellow and check out his story. I will be on my way. Please try to delay him."

"Will do. Hurry please."

Deputy Luke struck pay dirt. He was sure if the injury were not too severe the killer would come to the local hospital. He was right.

When Deputy Christy arrived at the neighboring county's emergency room, Sheriff Simmons had the fellow in handcuffs, sitting in the back of a cruiser. Simmons told the deputy, "That bear really got him. Yeah, three claws in the right shoulder, probably half inch in at the deepest."

"Are you sure it was a bear?"

"Sure am, Deputy. He told me it was a bear. He said it had caught him by surprise when he was hiking. I noticed blood under his fingernails on the right hand and asked him about it. He didn't have an answer to that. I had the nurse remove samples for you. I think they will be of interest to the DA."

"Thanks much, Sheriff!"

"My pleasure, Deputy. Just a little payback for the time you caught that kidnapper for us."

Luke smiled. "Thanks again!"

Deputy Christy transferred the subject into his car and drove off into the night. "Do you know what, Lance?"

"No, officer, what?"

"You tried to get our witness a couple of times." There was no answer from the back seat. "Even if you had gotten her, we have a video of the murder. You are going down."

"Yeah? Even if I can't get out, there is someone else to take care of the witness. And I don't believe you. I didn't see any cameras."

CHAPTER
— 10 —
THE PROFESSOR'S DISCOVERY

PROFESSOR JASON SAVAGE sat at the computer desk he had purchased from Adam Barnes, analyzing the code he had programmed into the software. He hoped the audio and video data he gave Sheriff Michaels was everything he was hoping for.

Jason virtually stumbled on the signal, some extremely fine, low-level radiographic interference in his lab. The interference had been distorting his readings and research and he was working on a graphic enhancement process for his systems. The original project was to use a very sensitive digital camera to pick up a secret message implanted in the video display of a high-density monitor. He had experienced limited success to that point.

Later that summer the professor stumbled across what

he would call the "universal frequency." As he focused his instruments on the interference, he isolated an almost unintelligible vibration well below the generally monitored frequencies. The discovery had been almost accidental. The most fascinating aspect of this vibration was that it came from virtually every solid object, and even some less than solid. It was particularly acute with crystalline substances. This frequency was universal—the universal frequency. The universal frequency showed no signs of independence. It was always riding piggyback, if you will, on other waves.

Once discovered, his challenge was to filter out the hauler waves, those on which the universal frequency was carried. He hypothesized, based on many of their characteristics, that there was a great deal of data for gleaning from the universal frequency. He was not sure what the nature of the data would be. It was very systematic and structured. It represented the structure of DNA. He reasoned, if the computing was processed within DNA, maybe the data released by exciting the atoms were also patterned after DNA. This being the case, he had to structure his receiver to read the digital DNA signal lying on a static wave.

It took Jason months to fine-tune his hardware and software configurations. There was a great deal of failure and frustration on his way to figuring it out. But once he did, he was able to pull video from the universal frequency. The video seemed random and confusing, especially after the audio started coming through.

During a flash of success, Jason had pulled the video

data into focus. In the middle of the focus was a clock with a sweeping second hand. He used that to establish a standard for the time within the videos.

At one point he stumbled across a library with a calendar on one of the tables. The date read January 27, 1932. This date became the anchor date. Using his twenty-four-hour calculation, he was able to determine what day, month, and year were being displayed and heard. This was the beginning of the revelation.

The proof in the data from this universal frequency was what Jason knew the sheriff needed to convict the murderers of Miss Austin.

CHAPTER 11
FORBIDDEN

IT HAD BEEN a couple of months since Deputy Christy caught the suspected killer, Lance Angie, and it was still months from the beginning of the trial. Marti and Adam had been living comfortably. He went to work. Marti had taken up gardening, and between that and reading, she had turned his rather plain property into a flowering sensation.

They had gotten used to having coffee together on the screened porch in the back every morning. On the days when the store was open, he left her in her robe, or less, as he walked out the door headed for the garage.

Marti had regained her confidence and was able to operate on her own in most situations. She used Adam's bike to travel wherever she wanted. She was a very solid money manager. She had invested the monies from her parents' estate in mutual funds and CDs. She always had money to do what she wanted to do, and that took pressure off Adam and his "new store" income. And they had become close friends.

Adam regularly struggled with the sexual tension between them. There were times when she did not wear modest clothes. There were too many chances to catch a glimpse of her beautiful body. He thought she knew what she was doing. But she did not make advances, and he behaved himself. There were times they would be very close, and Adam was sure she knew of his interest. And her interest was clear to him.

Marti had earned Adam's respect in many ways. She learned how to manage the trauma she had experienced. She had cleared her head and regained her direction. She was ready to go back to school—if she could live with Adam, which she said in a humorous way. Still, he thought there was a lot of truth in her statements. Marti taught herself how to laugh again, and he loved to hear her laugh.

She understood the meaning of responsibility. She regularly thanked Adam for letting her live with him until the trial was over. Marti took on her share of tasks about the home and helped him remember obligations and to relax. He was so proud of her.

Marti handled awkward situations with grace and style. If they were out shopping and someone asked if she were his daughter, she would grab his arm, pull herself in, and say something like, "Naw, I'm just his pal," smiling the whole time. If someone were looking at Adam in a clearly judgmental way, she would often say something like, "Hey, Dad, thanks for your help." Then she would look at him with a huge twinkle in her eyes. She knew he hated being called her dad.

They had not talked a lot about the murder, just passing acknowledgments. Adam knew he would have to get her emotionally ready for the trial, and she would have to relive the horror. What he was really afraid of was what the defense attorney would do to her. He could do his best to ruin her credibility with personal attacks and accusations. And, "What about her medication?" Adam was really afraid the medication would cause considerable doubts.

CHAPTER — 12 —
UNIVERSAL COMPUTER

SHERIFF SAM MICHAELS thought, *I wonder how Jason discovered this technology of his? I think I will give him a call.* Sam retrieved his cell and dialed like someone from his generation, with one finger.

"Hello."

"Hello, Jason. Sam here."

"Hi, Sam! What's up?"

"Hey, I have been wondering if you could tell me more of how you started looking for your system. Can I come by and we talk about it?"

"Sure. It is almost lunchtime. Can you run through the drive-through and bring me a burger? I'll pay you when you get here."

"Will do."

"I will be waiting on a bench in front of the building."

Sam pulled into the parking lot, parked the car, and got out of the cruiser with two bags in his hand. "Ready to eat?"

"Hi Sam! Sure am." Jason was working diligently on his cell.

"What are you working on, Jason?"

"Oh, solitaire. I don't know why, but I play this all the time."

Sam handed Jason his bag and took a seat on the other end of the bench. They made small talk while they ate their burgers and fries.

"How have you been?" Sam asked.

"Pretty good. I am really having fun with this semester's classes."

"Great! It is always good to enjoy what you are doing."

"Yeah, it sure is. Now, you said you wanted me to tell you why and how I found the universal computer. You know I thought impressions and/or questions I had might have been directed by the subconscious or maybe some other force. I mean it was *the* subconscious, not *my* subconscious."

"Oh?"

"Anyway, you know I did a great deal of research on solid storage and rock crystals?"

"Yeah."

"Understanding how that works led to questions on how the process was powered and facilitated. This new quest got quite spooky."

"What do you mean?"

"I'll tell ya. It has been known for quite some time that

crystals store data. They can hold great quantities of it. However, they must have a constant power source to do it. Now if I wanted to use this great storage solution, how would I power it? I considered radio waves, microwaves, radiation, and more. None of them would pass muster when I considered all criteria.

"Then I was puttering with an oscilloscope program, and like an epiphany, I noticed the background clutter. It was everywhere I looked. It was something we always had to filter. Always. I asked myself, 'What if I don't try to filter it? What if I try to corral it, to understand it?' That was it!"

"The background noise?" Sam asked.

"Yep! It was the only constant that was constant."

"Wow!"

"Yeah. After months of playing and tinkering, I discovered how to harness the background noise. It is a constant power supply that is everywhere.

"So I had the storage device and the power supply. But unless there is a way to facilitate the gathering and organizing of the data, there is nothing." Jason sat straight, and a calm came across his face. He exhaled and smiled. He shook his head as if he could not believe what he was thinking.

"Here is where it really gets weird. I discovered parts of a computer that was everywhere … everywhere. It hit me like a ton of bricks. The computer was omnipresent. A god computer." Jason stood and walked slowly around the bench.

"I started thinking about the CPU. There are many types made of transistors, resistors, capacitors, and diodes. This one uses DNA for processing." He stopped and stared into the distance. The corner of his mouth began to form a smile.

"DNA processors hold almost unlimited potential for computing speed. They run parallel processes that run parallel processes, up to thousands at a time. Current mechanical computers run one at a time." Jason stood and said, "Follow me!"

He started running to the door of the building and up the stairs to his office. Sam trotted behind him. By the time Sam joined him in the office, Jason was standing next to a shelf filled with books. It struck Sam funny; he had books. His whole life was digital, huh?

"Come in, sir!" he beckoned Sam, and continued. "My mom would kill me if she saw what I am going to show you. Come over here."

Sam walked over to the bookshelf. Jason took his finger and drew it along the top of the shelf. A long dark line appeared when he pulled his finger away. "This is the universal computer."

"Dust?"

"Yep, dust. A large percentage of household dust is skin flakes—DNA."

"Wow!"

"Yeah! So that explains the potential for the universal computer. You know how it works everywhere?" Sam shrugged.

"Okay, somehow this DNA arranged itself into a computing structure and began to multiply. Have you heard of nanoscience?"

"Yes."

"The universal—DNA—computer is on a molecular level, which enables it to do far more than I ever imagined. This nano-computer creates great grids only molecules thick, and it spreads itself everywhere using countless methods. I am amazed every time I think about this."

"But how does it get so big to cover so much?"

"This dust on my fingertip can create a grid a mile square. Of course it is not physically connected globally. Where the physical connection is not universal, it is connected by the best wireless system anywhere."

"Oh wow!"

"Yep, and it is intelligently organized and dispersed."

"Intelligently?"

"Yeah!"

"Artificial intelligence?"

"I don't think so."

"What is it then?"

"I don't know. Maybe it's *who* is it?"

Sam's mouth dropped. He felt like he had been thrown off the building. But Jason was going on as if he hadn't just floated the greatest concept Sam had ever heard. He let him go on.

Jason looked Sam square in the eyes and paused for what seemed like an hour. He spoke, "Sam, I have never told anyone this." Still eye-locked, there was another long pause before he continued.

"As I realized the validity, I heard a calm voice say, 'Welcome, Jason.' I could not sleep for two days. I still don't know if that was God, the god computer, or who."

CHAPTER 13
PREPARING FOR THE TRIAL

THE SHERIFF WENT to visit the district attorney in preparation for the upcoming trial of Lance Angie and later his accomplice. Walking into the DA's office, Sam was greeted by Jennifer, the deputy DA.

"Hi Sam!"

"Hello, Ms. Jennifer. How are you doing today?"

"I'm good. You? We are looking forward to the evidence. Come on in. The DA is ready for us."

Entering the large office, Sam recognized the DA sitting behind his rather imposing, dark-maple desk. He leaned back in his chair and said, "Hello Sam. Great to see you."

"Thanks, boss!"

"I hope you have some good evidence for me. We want to nail this guy good."

"It is pretty good stuff."

"I understand you have some groundbreaking evidence," Jennifer interjected.

"Yes," the sheriff replied. "Our traditional evidence is *nearly* airtight, but this new technology is a slam dunk! Let's start with the traditional, and we will get to the new stuff later."

Over the next forty-five minutes, Sheriff Michaels went over the required reports, the murder weapon, and photos of the scene, DNA evidence, and pictures of all those involved in this bloody crime. Sam finished the traditional evidence presentation with, "This is Marti Lawford. She is the eyewitness we talked about."

"She looks like a nice kid."

"She is, boss. She is a sweet person. Now the main issue with Marti is the olanzapine she is on for her depression."

"Yes, that is a big, potentially defeating issue," the DA replied and continued, "So, tell me about this new technology."

"Will do! This technology is revolutionary. It has never been used in a court of law. Here, plug this CD into your computer."

The DA slid the disk into the computer slot, and the screen came to life. Over the next several seconds Sam, Jennifer, and the DA watched the horrible killing of Amber Austin. Then the screen went silent. After a moment of quiet, the DA spoke up. "Who was filming the scene? The swinging of perspective was amazing."

"You know, boss, there were no cameras or mics in that room."

"What?"

"That's right. This new technology draws video and sound from the walls and such."

"What?"

"Yep. I will have Jason Savage, the inventor, explain it to you. It is really interesting. Make sure you book at least three hours. He will overwhelm you with information. But that is an actual display of what happened."

"There is no question that if this is real, it will remove reasonable doubt," Jennifer said.

"That's right," the DA agreed. "I think I'll withhold the new technology for the trial. We have enough for the arraignment. If it is admissible."

CHAPTER 14
THE ARRAIGNMENT

"**ALL RISE. THE** Honorable Robert B. Baughman."

His Honor ("Judge Bob" as everyone knew him) entered the courtroom. "You may be seated," he said. He stood there for a minute to see if anyone would remain standing. No one did, so he shrugged and sat at the bench.

The DA had not scheduled a time for Jason to explain the new technology. He wondered how Sam was so sure it would be admissible. Sam had not shared with him his and Jason's visit in Judge Bob's office, when they asked the judge to admit this new technology as evidence in the murder case.

* * *

Three weeks earlier, the sheriff stopped by the courthouse with Jason Savage in tow. He was there to see Judge Bob. Sam swung open the front door and headed to the left and down the long, walnut-laden, dark woodwork hall, past several open office doors to the one that said "Judge Baughman. He knocked three times.

"Come in, Sam."

"Hi Bob. Got a minute?"

"Doesn't look like that matters, Sam."

"Thanks! Now Bob, you know I have this kid down at the jail accused of killing the Austin girl."

"Yep. His arraignment is a few weeks out."

"Right. Well Bob, we are about to make history here."

"What do you mean, history?"

"I'm about to tell you we have an airtight case here. I got the killer and his sidekick."

"If you have such a good case, why are you here?"

"Like I said, we are about to make history. We have a new technology that Jason here ... Oh, forgive me, Bob. This is Dr. Jason Savage from the college."

Stretching toward Jason, Bob shook his hand. "Oh yes, Dr. Savage. I have heard a great deal about you. Welcome to Kingman!"

"Thank you, sir. Please call me Jason."

"Okay then. Jason, welcome!" Jason nodded in response.

"As I was saying," Michaels continued, "this case is airtight with the evidence Jason has been able to bring to bear."

"What evidence is that?"

"I thought you told me months ago that the Lawford girl was the only witness."

"She is. But we have more."

"Oh?"

"Yep, airtight … If this evidence is admissible."

"Okay, Sam, let's see it."

Jason started clicking on his laptop. The screen filled with the image of a room, the room where the murder took place. "Here goes," he announced.

Over the next few seconds, Jason showed the judge the evidence, in detail. He then stopped the program.

"That is unbelievable! How does it work?" Bob exclaimed, a bit shaken by the brutality of the scene.

"He has tried to explain it to me," Sam answered, "but I can only understand the basics."

"I can't admit that. It is unproven!"

"I thought you might say that, so we brought a little proof that might convince you to rethink your decision," Jason said. He turned his laptop toward the judge, clicked a couple of times, and looked at the sheriff.

"Bob, you ready?" the sheriff asked.

"Yeah."

"Go ahead, Jason."

One more click, and the monitor lit. Bob looked at the screen, and his mouth dropped. He watched for a minute or so and said, "That's the Sapphire Café. Bunny and I used to go there."

Sam looked at Jason. "Bunny was Bob's wife," he explained. "She passed a couple years ago."

"There she is!" Bob rejoiced.

Sam continued. "The date and time at this address was when we met to celebrate her birthday."

Just then Sam walked into view, followed by two other couples.

Bob erupted. "How did you get this video? I don't remember anyone taking one."

"That's the beauty of this technology, Bob. It gives us audio and video without any cameras or recording devices."

"What? How do you know it is real, Sam?"

"Do you remember this night?"

"Yes."

"Let's look in on what you two were talking about. What you talked about is only known by two people, you and Bunny."

"Okay," Bob said as he watched the screen.

Jason spoke to the computer. "Get closer to Bob and Bunny." The perspective of the video changed, moving closer to the couple and then closer, to their faces.

"Bob, I am looking forward to a good stiff drink."

"Me too, Bunny. Today has been a long one. Yep, but you look gorgeous tonight! Happy birthday, baby!"

"Aw, Bobby, you are the best."

"What are you going to get?"

"I think a Captain and diet, to start," she said. "Bobby, later let's sit in the hot tub." Bunny ended with a coy smile and a wink.

Jason sent a command and the screen went black. Bob sat back in his chair and sighed. Sam leaned in and asked Bob, "Did anyone else know what you two talked about?"

"No. We were almost whispering."

"Was there a camera in front of you two that night?"

"No. It must be real. There is no other way. No one knew what we were saying, and no one could have seen her wink. I am going to let this be admissible." After a long pause, "Can we go back and see her more?"

"Of course we can," Jason assured the judge.

"Let's do that later," Sam suggested.

"Good thinking, Sam." Bob said. "I will be waiting. That was an experience I thought I would never see again. I think I could even smell the steaks cooking."

Bob bit his lower lip, hit the eject button on the CD, slot and pulled it out of the computer. While handing the CD to Sam, Bob said, "That looks like pretty solid evidence to me. Your evidence will be admissible. But how do we get the jury to believe it?"

"We don't know right now," Sam replied.

"Even if you can convince this jury, our ruling is appealable."

* * *

The DA stood to begin the arraignment. He began laying out the evidence, which included photos of the crime scene, testimony, and DNA. The judge's ruling came right after the presentation. There was sufficient evidence to call a grand jury.

The grand jury later indicted the young man, charging him with murder in the first degree.

CHAPTER
— 15 —
THE MOTIVATION

SAM MICHAELS POINTED his cruiser toward the city hall to meet with the DA. As he drove, he thought back on nearly the six months since that horrible night when Amber Austin lost her life to stupidity and since Adam hit Marti with his car. A great deal had happened. Sam watched as the town got excited about the trial. This town has forgotten the viciousness of that night. It has taken on the spirit of a fair, a mystery party.

Sam thought back on he and his deputies working with the state troopers to build a good case based on Marti's eyewitness account. The physical evidence, the background, and the DNA evidence were also strong.

In the time since Sam had been sheriff, nothing like the murder and upcoming trial had happened in Kingman. *This should have been wholly tragic and sad*, he thought. *But this town shows great interest in the process. Many of the townspeople and students have followed events with great interest.*

Sheriff Michaels watched as people shared their thoughts and conclusions about the murder, the murderers, and the evidence—at least that which was public. Even the college offered a special course on the event.

Sam pulled into his spot at the city hall. He walked into the DA's office and asked the receptionist, "Is he in there?"

"Yes, go on in."

As he entered the DA's office, he said, "Hi, boss! I have some more background on one of the suspects."

"Great, Sam! Come in and sit down. What have you got?"

"Margaret Mason came up with the plan herself. I also have some motivations for her wanting Amber dead."

"Great! Go on."

"It seems that Ms. Margaret Manson, our accomplice, is the vindictive type. After a great deal of interrogation, she admitted to holding a grudge against Amber since middle school. Apparently, the grudge was based on envy.

The Austins, though not extensively rich, were quite well off. Margaret's family was on the poorer side of things. While Amber was generally well liked, Margaret's massive insecurity was apparent. She told several people how Amber acted all 'stuck-up' and rude.

"A little over a year ago, the old, one-sided, rivalry reared its ugly head when Amber made the cheerleading squad. Ms. Manson, who was already on the squad, had been outvoted. As shallow as this is, it is the motivation for the killing.

"Our witness, Marti Lawford, did not recognize Manson until her background was published in the paper. Marti did not really remember Manson, even though they grew up together in the same small town. Manson's family moved when the girls were in seventh grade. It apparently had been a tough time in her life, losing her father and having to move to another town to live with grandparents."

CHAPTER 16
THE TRIAL BEGINS

JASON RECOGNIZED MANY in the courtroom. Some were customers, and some were neighbors. There were also many folks he did not know. Most had dressed up a bit out of respect and the knowledge that cameras would be around. There were law enforcement there, including Sam and Luke. Jason saw two priests. There were four soldiers and two stiff-looking men in black suits with their hats on their laps. The local and regional TV stations had representatives with mics and cameras.

The scene was hushed with whispers reaching out from all directions when the bailiff called out, "All rise! Hear ye! Hear ye! The Honorable Robert J. Baughman of this session of the eighth circuit, calling to order New York State vs. Lance X. Ainge!"

With the court in session, the judge took several minutes to instruct the court and the jury.

The jury consisted of eleven women and one man. The average age of the jurors was approximately forty-five years old. Among the members of the jury were two teachers, two administrators, one doctor, one farmer, a domestic engineer, a pharmacist, a cashier, a professor, and a volleyball coach.

After setting the rules for the trial, Judge Baughman looked out at the courtroom filled to overflowing with people he knew and some he did not. He scanned from side to side and front to back. It seemed to take an hour. There was not a noise when he finally asked, "Mr. District Attorney, does the prosecution have an opening statement?"

The DA rose to his feet. "We do, Your Honor."

"Proceed."

Turning to the jury, he stepped from behind the prosecution table and strode slowly toward the center of the front row of jurors. He spoke slowly. "Ladies and gentleman, we have gathered here today to exercise a part of our society that wards off anarchy and lawlessness, which stands as a light for us to gather around and in which to believe.

"A tragedy has taken place in our town similar to tragedies that have happened since Kane killed Abel. Here, as in the case of that first taking of life, God requires consequences for the wrongdoer. Here in our town a life has been taken. That young woman is not here to speak for herself. None of us can help her. Her life was taken away from her and her family."

The DA turned and slowly raised his arm to point toward

Amber's mother, father, and sister. He turned back to the jury with glassy eyes, his pointing finger shivered in either rage or sympathy.

Stepping away from the jury box, he returned to the table, opened a folder, and pulled out an 8 × 10 photograph of a smiling Amber Austin. As he moved back to the front of the jury, he softly and slowly said her name. "Amber Austin ... remember her name. She is not here. She never, never will be." He raised her picture close to the jurors' faces, turned it to himself momentarily, and then back to those who would decide.

"Her name was ... was Amber. We cannot do anything for Amber, but we can make sure the lawlessness that cut short her life has consequences. With the joint efforts of my office, Sheriff Mathews, and our fine state police, we have evidence proving the one who drove the knife into Amber's chest and the one who deserves consequences for his lawlessness is that man right there, Lance X. Angie." He spun around to face the defendant with his arm extended. And this time, solid and steady as a rock, his finger identified the defendant. Ladies and gentleman, you are going to be ruling on conventional evidence and evidence based on new technology. As we present our case, the inventor of this new technology will explain it to you."

In a dramatic swing, the DA spun and pointed again at Angie. "This man thrust a six-inch blade through Amber's heart. Today we have evidence that will prove, beyond any reasonable doubt, that Mr. Angie is guilty: Amber is not here."

With that, the DA returned to his seat.

"Mr. McPherson, does the defense have an opening statement?" the judge inquired.

"We do, Your Honor." He stood, turned, and walked directly to the front railing of the jury box. "Ladies and gentleman," he began, looking straight at the only man in the box, "of the jury, you have just heard our beloved DA deliver a solid and confident opening statement. We, the defense, now open with humility and the determination to give you plenty of evidence and information to deliver the only verdict that can be delivered, not guilty by reason of reasonable doubt." He returned to his chair, and before sitting said, "Thank you, Your Honor."

CHAPTER — 17 —
THE PROSECUTION

FROM WHERE HE was seated, Jason could see everything that was going on in the courtroom. He adjusted his only tie. *This thing is choking me,* He thought. *I can't imagine wearing that suit and tie and a robe.*

Judge Bob hammered the gavel. "Mr. DA, the courtroom is yours."

The DA stood and again approached the jury box. "Folks, I am about to present a volume of evidence that, as I said, will remove all reasonable doubt that Mr. Angie, the defendant, and Ms. Manson, his accomplice, planned the attack on Amber Austin, resulting in the defendant killing Amber. I will seal the evidence with a video of the murder."

"I object, Your Honor," interrupted McPherson. "There were no cameras or microphones present at the murder scene!"

"Overruled."

"Your Honor!"

"Overruled. I told you this new technology would be admissible."

The DA continued, "Should you be unclear about any item or issue presented, please tell your foreperson, so we can apply the necessary time to clarifying the issues. I would like to call my first expert witness. Will Dr. William Dee come forward?"

Judge Bob spoke, "Dr. Dee, please come to the witness stand so the bailiff can swear you in."

"Please place your hand on this Bible," the bailiff began. "Raise your right hand. Do you swear to tell the truth, the whole truth, and nothing but the truth so help you God?"

"I do."

After the swearing in, the DA, turning again to the jury, continued. "Please remember, a great degree of this evidence will be scientific. It will be up to you to translate all of it and decide that Lance Ainge murdered Amber Austin."

"Objection! Drawing conclusions for the jury."

"Overruled."

The DA turned back to the witness. "Dr. Dee, would you state your name and address for the court?"

"My name is Dr. William Dee. I live at 24355 Central Avenue, Albany, New York."

"Thank you, sir. Can you tell the court what you do for a living?"

"Yes sir. I am a psychiatrist."

"How long have you been in practice?"

"I am in my thirty-third year of practice."

"Have you studied the records of our witness Ms. Marti Lawford?"

"I have, and I have had two sessions with her."

"Would you give the court your opinion of Ms. Lawford's diagnosis and her past and current conditions?"

"I will." Dr. Dee turned to face the jury better. "Ms. Lawford is a healthy young woman with some mental and emotional trauma experience. My diagnosis for Ms. Lawford is moderate depression, single incident. Ms. Lawford presented with a much-improved condition due to time and counseling."

"Dr. Dee, what is that single incident you are referring to?"

"Ms. Lawford, Marti, lost her family in an automobile accident almost two years ago."

"Has Marti's extended family been helping her with the loss?"

"It is my understanding that she has only one great aunt, who lives in California and does not know Marti."

"She is on her own then?"

"Yes, that is correct."

"How is she doing?"

"She is doing very well. She is a remarkable young woman."

"Objection!" McPherson blurted out. "That calls for the witness to make a judgment."

Judge Bob made an, 'Are you kidding?' face at McPherson. "Overruled."

The DA continued. "Please continue, Dr. Dee."

"She is a remarkable young woman. Considering the

trauma she has experienced, she is doing very well. Her mood is almost normal after such a short period. She is strong."

"Would you say she is a credible person?"

"Beyond a doubt."

"Thank you. I have no further questions for this witness, Your Honor."

"Mr. McPherson, do you have any questions for the doctor?" the judge asked.

"Yes I do, your honor. Dr. Dee, how was Ms. Lawford's mood six months ago?"

"I do not know. I had not met Marti then."

"No further questions, Your Honor."

The judge dismissed the witness and announced, "The court will take a fifteen-minute recess." He hammered the gavel and stood.

As the courtroom emptied, Jason was startled as a voice called, "Dr. Jason Savage?"

"Yes, I am he."

"Agent Randolph, Special Forces, US government."

Jason turned to see a tall man who appeared to be in his later thirties. Beside Agent Randolph stood another man, who was probably somewhat younger. Both men wore perfectly pressed black suits and ties and had cleanly cut hair. Each agent stood ultimately erect. The men's shoes carried a military-grade shine. Both agents carried a hat in their left hand.

"Hello, Agent Randolph."

"This is my partner, Agent Haws."

"Do you have some identification?"

They both held their IDs up for Jason to read.

"Thank you, gentlemen. How may I help you?"

"We have been asked to talk with you about your new technology that has been in the papers lately. We were wondering if you might have some time after the session ends today?"

"Yeah, I think so. Is there a problem?"

"Let's just say we have been asked to deal with this situation. Let's say six o'clock this evening at your office?"

"Sounds good. My office is at—"

"That's all right, Dr. Savage," interrupted Agent Randolph. "We know where it is. Six o'clock it is."

The agents turned and walked away. Jason turned as he began to wonder what they were looking for. All kinds of things went through his mind. *Do they want my secrets? Do they want my laptop? Do they know about the universal computer? Are they going to tell me to stop accessing it?*

He decided to try to calm down and not be paranoid. Just then Sheriff Sam Michaels tapped Jason on the shoulder. Startled again, Jason spun around like a top.

"Why so jumpy, Jason?"

"I guess it was those two agents."

"Yeah, I saw that."

"Why do they want to talk to me. They are coming to my office at six o'clock tonight."

"Would you like some company?"

"Oh yes, please!"

"No problem. I had marked them as Feds. They usually don't come around unless they need something."

"You know, Sam, I think they have been following me."

"I wouldn't doubt it. We will see what they want at six."

*   *   *

As it turned out, Judge Bob was not feeling well. An aide came into the courtroom about twenty minutes after the recess and told the attorneys Bob would be unable to continue today. She told the prosecution and the defense that the judge had remanded the jury to their room for the presentation of the new technology. She adjourned the court until ten o'clock tomorrow.

CHAPTER
—— 18 ——
CONVINCING THE JURY

THE DA AND Mr. McPherson joined the jury in their room a few minutes after the adjournment. The DA said, "Ladies and gentleman, you are going to be ruling on conventional evidence and evidence based on new technology. The judge has set aside this time for us to explain it to you. I am going to ask the inventor to come and give you an orientation."

Jason entered the room and walked to the end of the table, his red hair flaring. He took a minute to look at the jury before he began. "Ladies and gentleman, it is very unusual for a layman like myself to address a jury directly. With that said, I am very pleased to tell you, you are about to experience a new level of evidence, one that has never been presented in a courtroom before. In preparation for you to be able to rule on this, I have an unusual request. I need each of you to determine a date, time, and place or address where you experienced something no one else knows about. We can then begin going over this new technology in a personal way. Do your best to relax. I am going to explain this as succinctly as I can.

"The universal computer is a worldwide processor. It is not wired to anything. I don't know how it was created or by whom or what. It is based in microscopic DNA. That means it does not process one question at a time; it can compute millions of processes at the same time. It stores its data in crystals around the world. Its power comes from static electricity and transmits and communicates over a wireless system by means of micro-radio waves. If you have specific questions, I will try to answer them.

"We are among the chosen few who will rule on this new type of evidence, evidence that has not existed until recently. You will join those in history who have first ruled using things like fingerprints and DNA.

"Is this a valid form of evidence to rule on? Most people, after a short demonstration, are completely convinced of its validity. You will each go through the same type of verification process. Earlier I asked you to determine a date and time something happened that only you know about. Are you ready?

"The new evidence consists of audio and video at a location without any recording devices. I was fortunate to have some breakthroughs. The universal computer is everywhere and records everything.

"Sounds silly, huh? Yeah, I thought so too—until it proved

its existence and capabilities. This is where that date, time, and place we talked about earlier today come into play. I asked you to pick an experience only you knew about. I want to make this as interesting as possible. First, did any of you select a personal moment that cannot be shared?"

Everyone looked around, and two people raised their hands.

"I see there are two of you who will be uncomfortable sharing. Please try to think of another time. We will put you two last to see if you have time to think of another experience.

"Now, I want each of you to take your pads of paper and briefly write down what happened in your experience. We will compare your notes with what we see and hear with this technology."

Jason connected to the big flat screens on opposing walls. He looked around the table. "Let's get this going. Do we have any volunteers to go first?"

"I'll go first," a woman in her mid-sixties spoke up.

"Great! What is your name?"

"My name is Debbie."

"Okay, Debbie. Did you write down what happened on the date and time?"

"Yes I did."

"Okay. What was the time, date, and address?"

"It was 1977, December 24, at 7:15 p.m. I don't have the exact address, but it was at the Holiday Inn in Uniontown, Pennsylvania, in the restaurant."

"That's okay, the system will determine the address." The data entered, the screen slowly came into focus. The restaurant was dimly lit. Tables dotted the main floor, and booths ringed the floor. The walls and booths were decorated with tiny strings of lights. Tinsel and bulbs were hung everywhere. Christmas carols filled the air in a smooth, soothing way.

"Tell me, Debbie, what do we need to focus on?" Jason asked.

"That booth on the left end."

The universal computer had already begun to change perspective and draw closer to the couple in the booth. They did not seem to be enjoying themselves. The conversation seemed stilted and drawn. The perspective then moved to the center of the end of the table. The young man asked, "Do you think Bridget will bring her homemade bread over tomorrow?"

"She always does."

"I hope so. I love that bread!"

Debbie broke in. "Can we move ahead, to the end of us eating dinner?"

The system blurred the screen and began to clear it again. There were plates with the remnants of lobster tails and steaming cups of coffee on the table. The young man said, "I have a question for you, Debbie."

"Okay."

"Will you marry me?" He pulled a box from his pocket and opened it, displaying a single-stone engagement ring. He held it out to her.

She paused in an uncomfortable moment of silence before answering, "Yes."

He pulled the ring from the box, and with a shaking hand, pushed it onto her ring finger. They sat quietly and smiled at each other.

"That's good," Debbie said.

"Okay," Jason said and closed the connection. "Now let's compare what we have just watched with what you wrote down."

Debbie picked up her tablet and read, "My time and date are December 24, 1977, at 7:15 p.m. The address is the Holiday Inn, Uniontown, Pennsylvania. This was the night my late husband asked me to marry him. After dinner he will offer me his ring. I will say yes." She paused and smiled. "It was wonderful to see him again. That is exactly what happened."

There was a collective gasp among those in the room as the reality of the credibility of the system was acknowledged. The jury shared glances and nods. Eventually all eyes gathered on Jason.

"Thanks, Debbie! I am glad you got to see him again. Is there any way anyone else would have the information we just played for you?"

"No. I am the only one who would remember that time. The detail was amazing."

Over the next few hours, Jason continued and finished the personal verification presentations. There were less and less surprises as more of the jurors experienced what they remembered. The final two jurors did not come up with an experience to use to prove the system's reliability. Most said they believed in the technology. But Jason worried about the confidence levels of the two who had not experienced reliving their own memories.

CHAPTER 19
MEETING THE AGENTS

JASON GLANCED AT his watch: 5:44. *I wonder what they want? They will be here in less than a half hour. What am I going to do if they ask me to cease my research?*

There was a recital at the college, and all the parking was jam-packed. Jason finally found a spot about three blocks away. He jogged toward the office, where Sam was waiting at the front door. Soon the two agents joined them, and they all went inside to Jason's office.

When they were inside, Jason noticed Agent Haws point at a poster on the wall and whisper something to Agent Randolph. They shared smiles. Jason felt a bit better. He started to introduce the men. "Agent Haws, this is Sheriff—"

"Sheriff Sam Michaels," Agent Haws finished Jason's

introduction and continued. "Sheriff, this is Agent Randolph. We have been sent here to secure the situation."

"What situation is that?" Sam asked.

"Well, you see, Sheriff, Dr. Savage here has opened a can of worms."

"He has? What is this all about?" Since finding out about Jason's discovery, he had a feeling the news of what he could do would bring government sniffers. But little did he know the whole world was coming to Kingman.

"In case you haven't thought about it," Agent Randolph continued, "if this stuff works, whoever gets it wins. We have reports that Russian assets are on their way here. I am confident it is not the only country who has an interest.

"We have a hundred agents on this. They are spread out to fit in. Dr. Savage"—

"Please call me Jason."

"Okay, Jason. We believe you are in danger. There will be agents close by at all times."

"What should I do?"

"Act normal. Continue with the trial. Be prepared. You may be asked to come with us to an undisclosed location at any time for your protection."

"I am pretty sure I won't want to do that," Jason responded.

"Okay. We will come up with something. Just so you know, this is not a joke. The players in this game are the best and are intent on completing their missions. In situations like this, where I have been involved, assets have been terminated before they can complete their missions. We are intent on completing ours."

A chill ran up Jason's spine. Many thoughts careened through his mind. *Oh, my God, this is serious. What is their mission? Other country's agents are here to steal it. I am the only one who knows how to use it. That means they need me!* He was panting, nearing panic at the bleak thoughts.

Just then, Sheriff Sam Michaels spoke in that assuring tone of his. "We'll be all right, Jason. We have lots of help."

CHAPTER 20
THE DA CONTINUES

HAVING CALLED VARIOUS experts to bolster the case, the DA was ready to call the two witnesses who had actually seen the murder: Marti and the universal computer. Judge Baughman called the court to order at 10:00 a.m. and the courtroom grew quiet. The DA rose to announce, "The prosecution calls Marti Lawford to the stand."

There were muffled gasps and Marti stood. Judge Bob instructed, "Please approach the bench to be sworn in."

After the bailiff had done his duty, Marti took the witness stand. She wore a dark-gray, pinstripe, fitted suit. The DA approached the stand. "Good morning, Ms. Lawford. Please state your name and address for the court."

"My name is Marti Lawford. I have been living at 5287 Ridge Road, Kingman, New York."

"Ms. Lawford, what do you do for a living?"

"Right now, I am a student at Kingman College."

"Where do your parents live?"

Marti was ready for the question. During witness prep with the DA, he explained this question. He wanted to ask it to encourage jury sympathy.

"My parents died about two years ago."

"How did they die?"

"A car accident."

"Was the driver drunk?"

"Objection! Relevance," stated McPherson.

"Move along, counselor," the judge ruled.

"This line of questioning speaks to the witness's state of mind," The DA replied to McPherson's objection.

"Overruled."

The DA continued. "How is the rest of the family handling this loss?"

"There is no rest of the family. I am the only child still alive."

"Do you have extended family?"

The judge cleared his throat. The DA understood it was time to move on from the sympathy-gathering questions. Marti shook her head.

"Ms. Lawford, Marti, do you remember where you were the night of the murder?"

"Yes. I was at Amber's apartment."

"You were at Amber Austin's apartment. Is that correct?"

"Yes."

"Did you see the murder?"

"Yes."

"Can you tell the court what happened?"

"Yes."

"Please go ahead."

Marti nodded, took a deep breath, and began to speak in an emotional voice. "Amber and I were close friends. I had gone over to her place to discuss a hike we were planning for the following weekend. We were looking forward to it. We were going to climb Mt. Marcy. We were joking about running into a bear. We were laughing when a rock came through the window and hit Amber in the shoulder. She screamed and ran into the other room. I followed her. Then the door slammed open, and a guy came in. I think it was the new guy she had met."

"Objection! Hearsay."

"Sustained. Strike that from the record. Please continue, Ms. Lawford."

"The girl screamed at him to 'Get it over with!' and he went for Amber."

Marti was crying loudly now. She could get no words out. The DA asked Judge Bob for a few minutes. He granted the request and adjourned for fifteen minutes.

When the judge called the trial back to order, Marti was already in the witness stand. Judge Bob nodded at the DA, who stood and approached Marti.

"Okay, Marti. Continue. You said, 'He went to Amber.'"

Marti began with tears running down her face. "He raised

his hand and stabbed her with this big knife. She yelled and ran at me. She fell down in my arms."

Marti was crying loudly again. The DA looked at the judge and raised a hand, as if to say, "Hold on." Judge Bob nodded. After a minute or two, the DA softly asked Marti, "Are you able to continue?"

"Yes."

"You said she fell in your arms."

"Yes. I was so scared. Then he started to come toward me. I tried to run but the woman was blocking my way. I grabbed the desk phone and hit her with it. Then I ran out the door and down the driveway."

"Thank you, Marti. I have no more questions at this time."

"Mr. McPherson, do you have any questions?"

"I do, Your Honor." He rose from his chair, picked up a legal pad, and read it awhile before beginning. "Ms. Lawford. May I call you Marti? Can you tell me whose house is at 5287 Ridge Road, Kingman, New York?"

"Adam Barnes."

"How long had you known Adam Barnes when you moved in with him?"

"I had just met him. I—"

"Thank you, Marti," McPherson interrupted. "Next, did the man who you earlier pointed to stab Ms. Austin more than once?"

"I don't think so?"

"I don't think so. I'm not sure."

"Okay. Now were you on any medications at the time of the murder?"

"Yes."

"Which medicines were you on?"

"Olanzapine and Wellbutrin."

"Your honor, I would like to submit this definition of olanzapine from the *Physicians' Desk Reference*. It says, among other things, that this medication is often used with people who suffer from hallucinations. Submitted as defense exhibit 1. McPherson handed a copy to the judge. He slowly strode to the DA and handed him one as well.

"No further questions, Your Honor."

"Okay, Marti, you may step down." She took her seat behind the DA's table.

Slowly rising from his chair, the DA strode to the front of the jury box and took a deep breath. "The universal computer is a worldwide, all-encompassing processor. It is based in DNA and can compute millions of processes at the same time. It is the supercomputer of supercomputers. It stores its data in crystals around the world. It is powered by global static electricity and transmits and communicates over the airways by means of micro-radio waves. It knows what has happened and what will happen. It is the greatest, most reliable source of information and evidence. All of you have seen its reliability reproducing secret moments."

The DA looked at Judge Bob and said, "The prosecution would like to submit the following demonstration of recordings made by the universal computer, made on the date of the murder as exhibit 7 for the prosecution."

"So it will be. In what form do you anticipate submitting it?"

"It will be submitted as this DVD." The DA held up a CD in a sleeve as he walked a copy over to the defense.

"Proceed."

The DA walked over to the jury, CD in hand. Approaching the front railing of the box, he held up the CD. "Ladies and gentleman, I have here in my hand a new type of evidence, never before admitted to a court. In fact, it has never been seen by the public until this trial. This new evidence will be as important to solving crimes as the fingerprint. But this new evidence will do *more* than a mere fingerprint. It will do more than DNA. It will do more than eyewitnesses to solve crimes. How? This new evidence is recorded at the very moment the incident happened. It is an actual video with audio as recorded by the universal computer. This video is more reliable than any evidence has ever been. It has the potential to assure there will be no injustice or people sent to prison who did not commit crimes.

"This is a scientific epiphany, and you will be part of history. It is important for you to keep your perspective here because this earth-shattering technology will make sure justice is done for a sweet twenty-year-old girl whose life was cut short.

"On the three video screens here in the courtroom, everyone should be able to see clearly. If you are having any trouble seeing the video, please let me know immediately."

He looked over at Jason and nodded. Jason clicked on the

screen of his laptop. A scene of an empty living room formed on the screens. In the background were the sounds of two girls laughing. The sound of broken glass was followed by a scream of a girl, and Amber came running into the room. Over the next twenty-eight seconds, the horrific scene played.

"The prosecution rests."

CHAPTER
—— 21 ——
THE DEFENSE

THE COURTROOM WAS completely silent. A great number of people shuffled in their seats. Some fidgeted. Another bit his fingernails. Jim McPherson rose to his feet, and with brashness of arrogance, he began to speak.

"Ladies and gentleman of the jury, our fine district attorney has just laid out what I am sure he thinks is an airtight case. It lies primarily on three legs, like a stool. First, the testimony of an emotionally starved, traumatized, and ramshackle young woman. The second leg is DNA from under the fingernail of the boyfriend of the victim. Third, a leg based on computer-generated graphics. We will reconstruct a timeline that will show you the actual sequence of events leading to the murder of Amber Austin.

"The third leg of the DA's stool relies completely on

computer-generated graphics supplied by a young man hungry for approval and attention." Jason frowned at McPherson. "You can't rely on these computer-generated fairy tales. We will talk about this further.

The basis of the second leg, blood under the fingernail of Amber Austin's boyfriend. Per the prosecution's expert, the blood recovered from Lance's fingernail was type O positive, Ms. Austin's type. But the sample was degraded. Our expert will show you that it could have been someone else's blood, like his own.

"And the first leg of the DA's case is Marti Lawford, a young woman known for her unstable emotional behavior. Sure, she lost her family recently, but that was not when her irrational behavior started. It is amazing how she remembers so many details about Amber's murder. Don't you think she had exceptional details about my client's actions while in a horrendous situation? It seems to me it would be a blur for most of us. The district attorney's stool will fall to pieces when the evidence shows my client arrived at the scene of the crime as the mortal wound was being inflicted by the real killer, Marti Lawford."

There was an audible gasp in the courtroom. People were talking to each other and turning about.

Judge Bob slammed the gavel onto the desk four times. "There will be silence in this courtroom. Continue, Mr. McPherson."

The outline for the defense had been presented. It took Jim McPherson three days of minutia and allegations to confuse and worry the jury to his satisfaction. Hoping he had convinced at least one member of the jury that there was some semblance of doubt, he turned to the judge and announced, "The defense rests."

Judge Bob gave the jury instructions on their responsibilities and the process to follow. He sent them back to the jury room to deliberate.

It took the jury two days to reach a verdict. Angie was convicted of first-degree murder and faced a sentence of life imprisonment.

Marti completed her obligation to the process. She and Adam went home and happily struggled with their sexual tensions long into the future.

CHAPTER
— 22 —
THE TRINITY

A WEEK AFTER the trial, Jason sat at his desk and imagined what he was dealing with. When he first started discovering the miracle that would become an epiphany in the search for truth, he had no idea to where and to what extent the discovery would take him. Early on, with the sheriff, he had to place sensors on the walls where an event happened to get pertinent data. Now, many months after the pioneering efforts, he could draw data from anywhere and anytime without moving from his chair.

Sheriff Michaels asked Jason to meet with him again to continue his explanation. It was a nice day when they talked, and the window in Jason's office was open. The songs of birds came in through the opening.

As Sam walked through the door of his office, Jason greeted him. "Welcome Sam!"

"Hello Jason!"

"Oswald didn't do it."

"What!?!?"

"Yep. He didn't do it."

Sam stood dumbfounded in Jason's doorway. "You know if you go around saying stuff like that it'll make a lot of people happy. And a lot more people mad as hell." Sam was wrapping his head around at least one small part of what Jason had learned since their last meeting.

"Let me back up a little and catch you up." Jason offered Sam a bottle of water. Sam took it and slowly settled into a chair across the desk from the professor.

"I think I may need something a little stronger than this, but we'll see where it goes." He opened the bottle and took a long swig.

Jason had spent a lot of time grappling with the enormity of what he'd discovered and now it was time to bring Sam up to speed. But not too quickly. He didn't want Sam to think he was deep into some kind-of conspiracy theory rabbit hole. *Not too much technical detail,* thought Jason. Just enough to help Sam understand the concepts. He began. "Through the months I developed ways to interact with the universal computer. Then I realized it was time to investigate the source of the data. I had already thought the extremely detailed organization of the information, could not be random. I thought someone must have structured this collection system, storage system, and a power source. But there is no known earthly technology that could do that."

"So how was it structured?" Sam asked.

"Yep. I should have expected amazing stuff, but I was about to experience things almost beyond imagination. Remember, I heard the welcome?"

"Yeah."

"I told you about the search capability?"

"Yeah."

"So I decided to ask it, 'How are you structured and who built you?'"

"And?"

"This holographic bubble formed around my head, and the education began. I am going to summarize because the amount of information it gave me, I am still realizing. It was a voice-guided tour, which was pretty neat. It said, 'I am called Trinity. I am … the gathering of three.' 'First is the rock. All the long-term storage is held in crystalline structures around the world. Almost every crystal has billions of bits of storage capability. The whole world is covered with various types of crystals, all of which can store data. When the processor calls for data by exciting the electrons on the atoms of the crystals, vast fortunes are available to answer the request. The rocks cry out!' I thought about it, and then I remembered Jesus's entry into Jerusalem on Palm Sunday. I also remembered watching a TV show about haunted places."

Sam was shaking his head. "Okay, the rocks cry out and a TV show about haunted places. How does this fit together?" Sam asked.

"There was a place in Ireland, I think, where people went

to hear voices come out of the walls. At certain times of the day, usually after dark, it sounded like people talking and walking around. The words were unintelligible, but the walls were talking. What if it weren't haunted, and it was the crystals talking?"

"Wow!" Sam blurted out.

"Yeah, I know! Jason reacted and continued. "A while back I was sitting in front of a fire at my cabin. The flames were normal sized for my small fireplace. The flames were the only light in the cabin. I looked around and saw several of my rock collection sparkling in the light of the flames. You know, I have always thought crystals were a gift from God. I have always been enamored by the light they share with us. Crystals have always been intriguing. They are linked to mystery, energy, and the supernatural. For me, they inspire emotion and curiosity. As I sat there, the stones flickered and flashed. A thought spoke to me; these energies reminded me of eyes twinkling in the darkness. I wondered if this was just a random thought or maybe a truth. Who is looking at me? Why? I asked and meditated on these questions for a long time. Then another theory came. When souls pass from this plane of existence, they take with them a wonder about this world, a curiosity. Therefore, they search for opportunities to look onto this dimension. There are billions of souls searching. The Bible says they are a 'great host of witnesses.'

"Every once in a while, the conditions are just right for viewing. When light is available to light this world for them, souls position themselves to look through the faces of a crystal.

And we think it's simply a reflection of light. You know, people have always thought crystals have special powers. What if they really do, and the flashes of a crystal are eyes twinkling at us from beyond?"

Sam took a big breath. Jason wondered if he was accepting the explanation he was giving.

"Did you know I grew up in the church, Sam? The word 'Trinity' is familiar to me. According to the computer, this first part of the system—the crystals—it considers as the Son.

The second part of the universal computer is the processor. This is the part of the computer that gives direction to the power and the data. It is intelligence at the highest degree. It handles all live data. This processor is microscopic; comprised of DNA. The computing power of this arrangement approaches infinity. It is constantly growing it's computing capability. It is innate intelligence. Great sheets of the DNA processor are physically connected. Where they are not, the grandest wireless system bridges them together.

"These sheets of DNA are global in scope. When the processor processes data, it is moved to the static waves, awaiting requests. This is random access memory at its grandest." Jason looked at Sam as if to convey its importance. The computer said, 'I think of this second part of the Trinity as the Father.'

"Then the computer told me, 'And last is my power source, the universal frequency. It controls all the electricity in the atmosphere. It steers waves of all kinds toward a harmonic unity. It shepherds the static waves that hold the data.' We humans can sometimes perceive this one. It is most often known as background noise, the universal hum, or the roaring of silence. This one empowers the processor and enables the crystals to hold their memories. As I said, some humans can perceive this power source. They can tap into the real-time data held by the static waves. The computer said it called this the Spirit."

Jason turned to Sam, as if he had not just delivered a world-shaking reality. "Sam, I don't mean to shift gears so radically, but Oswald didn't do it!"

"Okay. What do you mean?"

"So many of us have always wondered who killed JFK. I remember my mom thinking talking and musing about it every time something came on the TV about the assassination. One day after my last class, I dialed in 'dallas, tx november 22, 1963 12:30.'"

"Wow!"

"Yeah! I expected the computer to take me to the grassy knoll or something. But it took me into a room where there was a table and a Coke machine. There was a person at the refrigerator. It took me a moment to realize it was Lee Harvey Oswald. He pulled out a small bag from the fridge.

"The window was open, and I heard *bang … bang, bang.* Just then someone came through the door, over there. I closed the machine. I haven't had time to go back, but, do you know what that means?"

"No"

"It means Oswald didn't do it."

"Jason, I am going through information overload. It may take me months to kind of get a grip on it all."

"You know, Sam," Jason continued as if Sam had not spoken, "I have some theories I have never told anyone about. I have been trying to balance the science and my faith. With all I have told you, you can imagine how those who don't believe will try to explain away God with the reality of this universal computer. So here are some of my theories."

"Okay. I am listening."

"There is a difference between science and the spiritual. That said, it seems we communicate with the universal computer and God in similar ways. We have all experienced the spiritual. Some try to explain it away, but we all know there is a spiritual realm. But how about our interactions with the universal computer?"

"What do you mean, Jason?"

"Well, because the universal computer's processor is DNA, there is a natural/scientific connection with living things. This connection with humans is fleshed out the same way radio transmitters and receivers work. Some humans are transmitters, some are receivers. The transmitters are those whose passions and thoughts are to a level that the universal computer cannot ignore. Thus, the result is that transmitters leave a record of what was most important to them. The universal computer stores this record and applies its version of emotion—DNA—to it. When this type of record is read, it appears and feels like a real person or spirit of a real person. There are different levels of transmitters.

"There are different levels of receivers as well. Some are at the scientific level. Many of these do not understand where they get the information. Examples of these are Einstein, Tesla, and von Braun.

"Einstein would regularly put himself into a trance, whereby he would gather data. He was such a good receiver, with his gifted mind. He changed the thinking of the entire scientific world.

"Tesla was particularly sensitive to the universal frequency. He understood the power in the air, but he did not describe it well. He did learn how to use the power and was killed because of this understanding.

"Werner von Braun was a tremendous receiver. He received and used the information to the great advancement of human exploration. His discoveries also made life on earth much more livable. How von Braun explained his reception of data unfortunately missed the mark. He thought he was receiving this data from extra-earthly beings.

"These three receivers often received the universal computer simulation results. This way inventions and discoveries were realized. Other receivers pick up information from the universal computer on an emotional and/or innate level. These folks will then have to interpret the emotions and passions differently. Examples of this type of receiver are Edgar Cayce and other clairvoyants, spiritualists, and sensitives.

"Edgar Cayce was a remarkable receiver. He used his trance-received data to answer hundreds of people's questions and requests. He was able to use the system's data and probability calculations to prophesize which horse would win a race and even what wars would come. He and some other receivers used the probability indicators sent from the universal computer to project what would happen. These would be seen as fortune-tellers or prophets.

"Some receive data on a more emotional level. These people are prone to pick up passions or desires from a transmitter who left a record. These are often misunderstood as souls trying to communicate with the living. I think receivers often pick up emotional transmissions from the universal computer that they interpret as memories. This type of reception tends to make people believe in reincarnation."

Jason stopped talking. He turned to Sam and asked, "What do you think so far, Sam?"

"So far? So far this is incredible. It is pretty powerful stuff!"

"Yeah, it is. I just can't believe I am the first one to look into and understand these things. I can't believe I am the only one who has wondered about the background noise and this extent of DNA processing. You know, it all makes me kind of nervous. I feel like I am playing at a level that is out of my league. I have to believe different governments have been working on this. But I am nervous about other countries wanting my system."

Sam had been drinking from a fire hose and was overwhelmed by what Jason told him. Jason obviously had been thinking about this a lot. It was going to take Sam a while to absorb it all. He decided it was probably time for him to get home. Sam stood up and shook Jason's hand. He shook his head, smiled, and headed for his car. Back inside, Jason wondered if Sam was worried.

CHAPTER 23
THE TECHNOLOGY

JASON COULD TASTE the acid in his mouth. He thought it must be bubbling up from his stomach. He was worried because he was about to run his technology for a person he knew nothing about and had never met. She called Jason after reading about his system in the Kingman *Gazette*. She left him a message, just like all the other dozens of people. The only reason he agreed to see her was that she said it was an emergency, and she had to see him. He decided to meet her at his office as he did not want to invite unknown people into his home.

Arriving at his office building, he stuck his key in the lock. The lock was not the original as the door was hung in place in the 1820s. It gave a rather large click as the deadbolt retracted. Jason swung the heavy door inward and stepped inside. The doormat was thick and coarse. Stepping on its bristles, his foot sank with a bit of a shifting feeling. He began climbing the five flights of stairs to his office door. Another lock, another key, and he entered. The unfinished floorboards creaked slightly, and the scent of the old wood surrounded him.

Jason walked to his desk, which sat in the middle of the space. Thumping his laptop case on the top, he sat in his ergonomically correct computer chair. Having opened and started his computer, he stood to walk down one of the great peaked aisles toward the great windows trimmed in stained glass. Below was the parking lot. Jason had asked the woman—Janice—to call him when she arrived at the college. Just then a car pulled into the lot and parked. Within seconds, his cell rang.

"Hello, this is Jason."

"Hello, Professor. This is Janice Shooster."

"Hi, Janice. I will be right down."

He slid his cell into his front pocket and felt it slide to the bottom. Heading out the door of the office, the floorboard squeaked again. He moved quickly down the steps until finally reaching the vestibule. He grasped the handle and pulled the door inward. There, standing before him, was a woman in her early thirties. She stood approximately five feet four inches. She was cute and had a charming upturned mouth. He reached his hand out to shake hers. Her grip was strong and rippled his knuckles.

"Sorry, Professor. My father taught me to have a firm handshake."

"No problem, Janice. My hand should straighten within a

day or so," he said with a chuckle. "Come on in. My office is in the attic. Will five flights of stairs be a problem?"

"No problem. Thank you for seeing me so quickly."

"You said it was an emergency."

"Yes, thank you! The article said all we needed was an address and the time when an event happened."

"That's right. I should be able to help."

Janice did not speak for the final five lengths of stairs. *She is not volunteering what we will be looking for.* Jason thought. *"I wonder why.* Following her, he could smell what he thought must be rather expensive perfume. At the top landing, she stopped.

I forgot how small this landing is. I almost can't get by. Sliding behind her, he could smell the freshness of her hair. He turned the doorknob and let her pass.

Jason offered Janice a seat in front of his desk. He sat behind. Looking at his laptop, he began to type and speak. "Let's get started. Would you like to tell me what we are looking for?"

"No, let's just see what happens."

That's weird. Why won't she tell me. "Okay. Do you have that address?"

"Yes. It's 2718 Knowledge Way."

"That's just a few blocks away."

"Yeah. I know."

Jason turned back to the computer and typed in the address. A house came into view. It was a brick, one-story home that fit nicely in to the cozy town. He turned his laptop toward Janice. "Does this look right?"

"Yes, that's the house," she said, nodding guardedly.

"Do you have a date and time for me?"

"Yes. October 9, at 5:30 p.m."

He finished entering the date and time. "I will start the time running now. Will we need to go inside?"

"Yes."

"Go inside," Jason commanded. The computer display faded from the front of the house to inside, looking into what was clearly a living room. There was some shuffling somewhere, but it was out of sight.

"Do you know your way around this house?"

"Not really."

"What are we looking for?"

"Can this thing move around the house?"

"Yes."

"Let's look around."

Jason felt uneasy about looking around someone's home without them knowing about it. He drew in a big breath and cranked his neck to the side. "I'm not sure …"

Just then two people fell out of a doorway, across the hall, and against the wall. A man and a woman wrestled in passion, removing their clothes.

"That's all I need, Professor," Janice said in a sharp, hateful voice. "How much do I owe you."

"There is no cost," Jason, shocked, said. "Who was that couple?"

"Don't worry about it. It's my problem." She stood straight

up, whirled around, and started for the door. "Thank you," she said as she flung open, passed through, and slammed the door.

Jason sat in shock. *What the hell just happened here? I guess that was her husband? That was not right. How could she?* He slammed the laptop closed. *I just intruded on somebody's privacy. I could have broken laws if they apply to this system. What do I do about this type of thing?*

Jason wondered if he should have ever developed this technology. *How many homes will I break up?* Then the finality of this struck home. *There are no more secrets.*

Jason packed up and decided to head home. Walking to the office door, the floor squeaked. Jason smiled. He started walking to his car. He thought, *This technology is unbelievable. I probably have fifty voice messages of people who want the same thing. It is so scary. These thoughts are so negative. I have to think positively.*

The reality that history would no longer hold mystery was palatable. Jason let his mind run with the possibilities. *I wonder how far back the universal computer will let us go. Could we see dinosaurs? I bet we can. What about did Hitler die in the bunker or get away? Who killed the Kennedys? Was OJ innocent? Did we know about 9/11 before it happened? There are so many things we can answer. There is so much justice we can assure, just like the justice we brought to the memory of Amber Austin.*

He was almost to his parking spot when a car's tires squeaked as it stopped short of hitting him. He continued walking the final few feet to his car. Just then the car's doors opened, and two men in black, each holding a gun, jumped out. Jason turned to run. *Bang!*

Jason felt a hard impact in the back of his head, and in the seconds before the light was gone and as the continuing weapons' fire faded, he wondered, *Were they the Russians? Who was it that welcomed me to the universal computer? Is my faith real?*

And then a warm white light surrounded him, and he thought with a fulfilling release, *No one else knows how.*

Made in the USA
Monee, IL
11 June 2023